PASSAGES

PASSAGES

A Voyage from War to Peace

P.K. EDGEWATER

PASSAGES

A Voyage from War to Peace

By P.K. Edgewater
Copyright © 2025

Paperback ISBN: 979-8-9929026-0-0
Ebook ISBN: 979-8-9929026-1-7
Library of Congress Control Number: 2025908682

First Edition

Cover and Interior Design by Kimberly Peticolas, www.kimpeticolas.com

10 9 8 7 6 5 4 3 2 1

*To veterans and those around them who
buffer the shockwave of war.
To my parents who, in love of country and faith in its
destiny, lent each of their children to its armed services.*

PROLOGUE

Verdant water gave way to richer blue as his father skippered the trawler *Selene* at a comfortable pace beyond the shoals toward San Georgios. The late May sun had soothed the sea's swells southeast of Salamina into a relaxed submission. The sound of the engine tappets set the mind to a steady rhythm as the craft motored smoothly forward, all tidy now after the morning's catch and delivery. Now the same working craft was a pleasure boat of sorts and seemed to behave with that demeanor.

"Miko!" Kostas's resonant voice was elevated now, the third shout breaking Miko's hypnotic state from the tranquil patter. "Son, finish the lines and fenders and come steer with me. I want to tell you about what we may see today at the island, and maybe we talk about some other things, too."

There was no resistance from Miko, warming in the solar sparkle of an ancient and fabled Aegean Sea. Kostas went along with his son's silent boasting; Miko deserved to be proud in his father's eyes. Kostas rewarded Miko with days like this for getting good grades in school. A bonding adventure, just the two of them, was in the making. Never one to think of the boat and the sea as just work, Kostas contrived the dual-purpose outings to claim Miko's attention. Somewhere along the day's journey, a seed or two of wisdom would pass onto ground made more fertile by self-esteem.

"Yes, Papa!" Miko piped up, as if a sailor responding to orders.

Kostas looked twice. The adolescent's vocal resonance had deepened since but yesterday, save for the occasional airy fluting in the evolving register of a late-blooming thirteen-year-old. Once in the cabin, Miko donned his replica captain's cap; a token to Miko of Kostas's pride for last year's creative writing award as he transitioned to middle grades. That it was becoming already too small for Miko's bushy head was mitigated by the ease with which Miko could now see the entire horizon as he stood at the helm, no longer needing Papa's lap. Stowing the trawler's heavy kit had become notably fleeter as his shirts filled out.

"Why are we headed toward San Georgios, Papa?" Miko chided. "Are we looking for the mermaids you once told me are the only beings that live there now?"

Kostas's eye-rolling could not mask the smirk across his mouth, acknowledging his own mischievous capacity for tall tales.

"There has been a small craft alert during the past three days, aimed at near sunset today." Kostas began. "Our Royal Hellenic Navy will be out from Salamis Island for target practice on some old tub just on the west side of San Georgios. We'll have to keep our distance, but I thought it might be fun for you to watch," Kostas explained. Although the identifying markings on the old ship were removed or painted over, the alert mentioned that the ship to be sunk was named *Nearchos*.

Indeed, this was something new. "You mean they are going to blow up another ship?" Miko wanted to clarify.

"Yes, something that we don't often get to see," Kostas affirmed with relish at the opportunity. He peered at Miko apprehensively out of the corner of his eye. Miko returned the identical cornered squint, conveying suspicion he was perhaps Papa's captive excuse for the voyeurism on the agenda that afternoon. The communication was lost on neither. Kostas had woven into their bond never to let Miko feel the less manly for having his mother's leanings toward pacifism and a progressive world. Miko reached out to his father's shoulder and gave a gentle push sideways. Their smiles for each other in unison settled any differences they might have had over the plan.

"Okay, Papa." Miko gently nodded his head. He was nearing eye-to-eye level with his father and had grown confident in being more direct. "What else is on your mind? Are you planning to ship me off to the Navy when I'm sixteen?"

"Miko," Kostas responded, squinting into the distant horizon, deftly signaling the shift to his wise mode. "Your mother and I are not blind," he paused. "We are not sure where it came from, but you do well in school. Your teachers say that you are exceptional among your classmates. They don't come right out and say it, but I know they think you should go further than most of the children. You and I have never really talked about this. Most fishermen around here want—well, really, expect—their sons and daughters to help them and take over the business as they grow up. I must tell you something now so you start thinking about it."

Kostas's eyes came back from the distance and focused on his son's silent face, the fixed gaze governing a gravid pause. Miko flushed, caught off-guard by his father's sudden pivot to earnestness.

"I am not a proud man, but I am a happy man. All I have wanted since I was your age was to captain a boat like this, be my own boss, and catch a lot of fish. But you—well, you may be meant for other things. I am telling you . . . ," Kostas's eyes searched both sea and sky for words. "I am telling you to do what you want, go where your heart takes you. Your mother and I will be fine. If you want to fish, that is fine, too. You have some time. But start thinking about it."

The wisdom had been passed, slipped like a fresh sardine into the banter of the afternoon. Miko kept a silent stare toward San Georgios. The engine patter and the sea gushing by the bow could sustain such a contemplative moment, particularly on a placid Mediterranean afternoon. Miko held back, embarrassed that he himself had not pondered this important stuff yet. How bright could he be, then, after all, he mused silently.

Kostas left it there. An answer was not needed. The two locked eyes for moment, each scrutinizing the other's face. Miko felt his father's exquisite gentleness, the love palpable in his patience. That quickly, their journey as father and son had transitioned to a new dimension. Childhood was nearing an honorable demise.

"How much do you remember about your Grampa Demetrius, on Momma's side?" Kostas asked Miko with a slight head turn, yet keeping eyes on the island ahead. "He passed away when you were about five, I think. Remember? He lived with us for a while when you were little."

The reach for memories drew down the corners of Miko's mouth, eyes squinting pensively. An image formed, surrounded by an aura of tension bordering on fear, an uneasiness embedded during the five-year-old's innocence.

"Sorry, Papa, I don't remember much, but what I do remember is not really good. Grampa Demetrius was fat, and his face was stubbly all the time. He seemed like just a grumpy old man. He seemed to sit around talking to the same old guys most days in front of the bistro down the hill or on the docks. I never really got to know him. I don't think he liked me. I seemed to be a bother to him and his friends. I don't think about him much, but when I do, it puzzles me."

"Well," Kostas paused a moment, "I understand. Yes, he was, as you say, grumpy to everybody but his old navy buddies from the big war. That was when Greece had a real navy, but it was small and got pounded by the Italians and Germans until we allied with the British navy. It's a miracle that your Grampa Demetrius or any of those old guys survived. They came back from the war with wounds to their bodies, their minds, and their souls. And they hung together, like they had a bond of mixed pride and shame. Demetrius never talked about the war around your momma and me. But then, he worked hard on the boats until he could no more, I can say that. It's not that he did not like you, Miko, he just had a short temper and would shout at anyone who didn't rise to his expectations. Momma and I got some of that, too. When we put him in the ground, even Momma cried that there was something about him she would never know or understand. I think we must not judge him too harshly. It is a mystery to the rest of us what war can do to a man, not just to his flesh, but to his spirit."

Kostas dropped anchor accurately at the two nautical mile perimeter from the naval range using his new and highly-cherished global positioning kit, the pinnacle of cutting-edge wonders in a common man's navigation in 2006. Mouth open, he squinted through vintage binoculars.

"Hmm, yes," as he passed them to Miko. "Focus best you can, one thumb to the east side of San Georgios. You should make out the target vessel—the bright, white one with no markings. Do you see? You can't miss it; the sun is making it glare like a mirror."

"I spotted it before you did, Papa," Miko made clear, already feigning binoculars by holding his hands curled in tubes over his eyes. He reached for the glasses and searched the horizon. "Huh!" the sighting evoked a gasp of surprise, the modest magnification bringing in more visual content than expected. "Jesus, Mary, and Joseph, it's beautiful. Papa, it's a beautiful ship!"

"'She's' beautiful, Miko—not 'it,' but 'she,' like our *Selene*," Papa instructed. "Worthy vessels are addressed as elegant ladies, with respect for how they take care of us. You know that! But tell me what you see."

"I don't know, Papa," the prize-winning novice scribe searched for words. "She's tall and proud. She has a sleek bow and stern that demand respect, like she could fly into battle." Miko giggled and shrugged his shoulders guardedly up, not letting go just yet of the "she" thing. "The bridge, well, is like a big bosom in a tight sweater and a choker necklace!"

Papa smiled and shook his head. No doubt where this could go if he let it. "Now, now. Look again, do you see the Navy ships lining up?"

"Yes, Papa, there are three of them. They are all different sizes. One has big cannons on each side." Miko paused as he scanned for detail. "The next has smaller guns, but still pretty big, up in the front. The last—I can barely make it out—is very low, almost flat. Do you think it could be a submarine on the surface? They are all heading away from us, curving away in a row, getting nearer to where the white one is; it's just sitting there. When do you think they will start firing, Papa?"

Before an answer came, a series of flashes issued from the bank of guns on the largest craft, followed by a muffled boom that rattled the trawler's wheelhouse windows. The glistening white target rocked slowly. Black smoke quickly emerged skyward in an expanding column.

"Papa!" Miko's voice cracked loudly. "Are you sure there are no people on that ship? Are you sure?" Miko let his arms rest at his side, trembling, unable to steady the binoculars for viewing.

"Of course, Miko! This is an exercise—target practice— not a real battle. The old vessel is empty and defenseless. This is for training the sailors, and it has always been one way to dispense with war ships at the end of their lives. It is okay!" Kostas assured.

The middling craft and then the submarine took their turns, both provoking columns of red flame from the midship and the bridge of the target. Kostas recoiled slightly, noting the silence that had fallen over Miko as the impacts piled on. Miko leaned closer to a side window, unable yet to fully hide his face, tightened and distorted, from his father. Eyes and nostrils moistened until the overflow rolled unchecked.

Papa draped a comforting arm about Miko's shoulders. Miko's reaction sought solace that could come no more gently than from this gesture, done in the father's man-to-man way, giving space for sorrow without shame. Ushering his own deep sigh, Kostas felt the rigidity in Miko's posture relenting, submitting to the natural order of things, in solidarity with the fated destroyer being fired upon.

Listing away from the island, the *Nearchos* bowed slowly forward to its spellbound audience, gushing air to the surface from its midsection, belching flame and black cloud from its wounds, then rose again. She paused, as if balance had been recovered, enough strength for one more moment to meet the eyes of the father and son, then laid resolutely to stern and slid aft with the grace of a natural inhabitant of the depths, the sea closing wistfully around where she had faced her executioners.

As the assailing vessels began an orderly withdrawal from view, Kostas cranked the engine to idle. "Show is over! Let's start heading back. Momma will expect us for dinner and will be in a tizzy if it is dark by then. Bring up the bow anchor; I will get the stern." Kostas commanded. "Step lively, lad! We can talk about the sinking on the ride back if you like. Your mother will want to hear, too."

Miko's face dried quickly, leaning into the action and the late afternoon breeze. He was his father's son; his focus on freeing the lines and stowing them along with his papa pushed other thoughts aside. In due course, the tasks broke the tightness in his throat. Writing had taught him to let emotions marinate a while before collecting the right words. Perhaps it was merely the physical act of applying pen to paper, or more recently, pecking the words onto the computers at school that would calm him, and allow for an organized flow of ideas to phrases in print. It didn't matter. He welcomed the nudge from Papa to emerge from the present unexpected funk.

The ride home always seemed to take forever. Kostas entertained himself with a baritone shanty about a pelican and an albatross that made no sense, a tune Miko hated, and knew it would probably play in his head all night. To shut Papa up would require conversation, loud and exhausting over the drone of the engine. Miko loved it all. In moments like this, he could imagine no better life. He wasn't in a hurry to grow up.

"So, Papa, what did you think?" Miko took the initiative, hoping that Papa's answers would not be too deep nearing the day's end.

"Power, my gosh! We got shaken from two miles away from those cannons. No wonder they can drive a shell through several layers of steel. Incredible to see that firsthand!" Kostas marveled. "How about you?"

Miko gazed at the eastward horizon broken with the contours of distant islets, avoiding the evening sun's glare at starboard. He moved closer to Kostas ostensibly so as not to have to shout over the engine noise.

"I can't get over it, Papa" Miko led off. "The ship they sunk, the *Nearchos* you called it. She looked so proud and shining, even in her old age. We just saw her go down. We know nothing about her life. Where she has been. Who was her captain and her sailors? Wouldn't that be interesting, Papa?"

PASSAGES

Miko's imaginings supplied a never-ending source of entertainment for Kostas. "That's what seems so powerful to me, Papa. What was life like for the *Nearchos*, and for those who sailed her?"

"I don't know how much information you can find on an old ship like that. Why don't you make up something about it for school sometime?" Kostas said, hoping to harness Miko's energy.

Halfway up the winding cobblestone road, the harbor's fishy smells at Vathi Village gave way to the aromas of souvlaki and sizzling shrimp intensifying as they neared home. On their arrival, Momma's face was frozen in the sardonic smile she applied toward sea-going embellishment, particularly in the telling of foolishness. Yet her men were home and happy, at last, and the wine was helping.

Sleep came easily after a day of sun and sea motion, capped off by a belly full of Momma's culinary inducements. Miko slumbered motionlessly before ascending through sleep's languid shores where the mind's odd perceptions pass unquestioned. Bringing to wakefulness the dream developed therein, Miko wanted to save this one. Going straight to his desk, he scribbled furiously lest the images fade too fast, until his bladder could wait no more. He was more alert with the relief, but the dream memory was already clouded. Back at the writing table, he picked up the paragraphs he had written to see if any of it made sense.

He remembered. Between the level where people sleep-walk and where they are still, he had relived the day before—with one stark exception. The questions that rushed through his mind as he had watched the naval artillery exercise had been rejoined in his dream state by the essence of the *Nearchos* herself. Gleaming again in the fugue, her conversation was natural and at ease. Miko put the day's rhetorical inquiry directly to the steely being before him and pushed to know of her essence and her story. Her enigma unfolded as she spoke to him.

"Stories are of the past, and the past exists only in thought."

"What about your past?"

"Memories don't matter. What matters are what we can draw from the universe of knowledge."

"What do you mean?"

"Humans are most curious. You contribute so much to the universe of knowledge, yet you are able to draw so little from it."

"I feel like my mind is going all the time!"

"But you fear change. My form does not resist change. I have no remorse, and no claim to permanency. I will serve as target practice today, as noble a purpose as any other. Whatever I become hereafter will still hold the essence of where I have been and of those whom I have carried. Take what is useful to you of my story, but bear me no sympathy."

"But who can tell me your story?"

"Ah! Men gave me a name, as if to make me human—even a gender as if I am their mother or their lover. This I get for keeping them from being consumed by the sea, as they surely would have been. Men fashioned me to kill other men. I take no blame. The killed men had stories, too—almost certainly the same ones."

"Are there still men who could speak for you?"

"Watch the gun boats align, testing the accuracy of the cannons and torpedoes, the timing and coordination to send me to the tranquility beneath the waves. Know there is a man who rode my back whose story tells as much as can come from words."

"And how would he tell of you beyond using words?"

"Be conscious; be patient. This is no journey of fantasy, but one as real as any notion you have held in your mind, its source untraceable yet no less profound."

Ψ

"Momma," Miko opened softly, approaching her from behind as she hummed, obliviously dicing the day's vegetables with her sharpest paring knife. There were times when it was fun to startle her; when she was armed was not one of them. "I wrote something this morning just after waking up, and I don't even understand it. Will you read it and tell me what you think?"

Miko stood still, reading his scrawl again to himself, noting now that what had seemed a meaningful conversation in his dream was barely intelligible. His mother concluded the staccato chopping and surveyed the countertop for the next task at hand before slowly turning her countenance and attention to her emerging man-child.

"Let's see what you've got," Sophia wiped her hands on her apron, taking a seat at the kitchen table. Her feedback meant everything to Miko. She had been the inspiration for his interest in writing and had nurtured his creativity, having briefly been a schoolteacher before marrying Kostas. She left that calling and the city to join the fisherman in Vathi. "Awake and writing this early on a Saturday?"

"Momma, it seemed so real! Just as I was waking up, I dreamed I was talking with that ship Papa and I saw yesterday. Isn't that so strange? It's funny—I remembered a lot just after waking up and started writing while it still made sense. But then it all seemed crazy. Read what I wrote. What do you think it means?"

Sophia took a seat at the kitchen table, sipped from her cup of tea gone tepid, gathering her own attention for the cognitive task. After a quick review, she leaned back in the chair, extending the page further from her face, and slowed her breathing for the reread. Finally lifting her penetrating eyes, she lay the paper flat and clasped her hands over it.

"Miko, this is puzzling," she began, "but I don't think it is nonsense. The ship was talking to you in your dream? Oh, my dear! It seems that your mind was trying to make some sense out of what you saw yesterday and place it into some larger picture."

"Okay, Momma, but what about the part about one man's story? What man?"

"Yes, Miko, I see that, and I have no idea." She said fairly. "You know, when I read something that I don't understand, but want to understand, I put it somewhere and come back to it later. Sometimes, much later, when something else reminds me of it, I come back and read it again. Then I may be able to put the meaning together. Why don't you put this somewhere for now?"

Still standing, Miko nodded, but put no motion to acting on her advice. Taking notice, Momma leaned silently again into the back of the slatted, sturdy wooden chair, drawing the still clenched hands onto her lap. She crossed her legs authoritatively at the knees, signaling her patience for what would come next and wordlessly welcoming Miko to sit and continue.

Miko indeed kept a notebook for such things he had written, and anything important on paper, on the shelf over his window. He had never had an occasion yet to question Momma's wisdom. But for now, there would be one more query.

"Momma, yesterday, when we were out there, Papa asked me if I remembered much about your papa, Grampa Deme-trius," Miko begin slowly, staring without focus at the paper on the table before them. "Well . . . See . . . I'm sure you loved Grampa, but, well, I remember him as kind of mean. I'm sorry, you know, I was a little kid; what do I know?"

Sophia nodded silently, giving permission. In her teaching days, she had honed ample skill in drawing out others' words by not blocking them with hers.

"My first thought about this puzzle from my dream is that the man may have been Grampa Demetrius," Miko went on, "so that, now, well, I'll never know what message, or what this riddle means or about the *Nearchos* since he is gone a long time ago."

Sophia remained silent, yet her eyes opened wider and more penetrating on Miko's face, her lips gently parted. Slowly, her palms rose to her cheeks as if on their own command, her fingers then sweeping gently to conceal her mouth and chin through one continuous motion. Miko shifted in his chair.

"Miko," Sophia paused. "Doing the math in my head, the ship that was sunk yesterday was old, but not old enough to be anything Grampa was on in that big war."

Miko squinted with eyes and lips, pensively nodding accord.

Sophia drew and held a deep breath before speaking. Only rarely had Miko or Kostas ever found her at a loss for words. Miko appreciated that Momma would be straight and treat him as intelligent, not in a pandering way. But as with Papa the day before, he felt the soft sand under their relationship shift to a new footing.

"I know my father, your grampa, loved me, even though he was grumpy. I always thought he didn't want to be mean, but he had little patience. There was a part of him I wanted to know better and never got the chance. My own papa," Sophia held her palms up in disillusionment, "and he seemed to be the one person that I could not get to talk to me. My momma died just before you were born. She used to say to me that Grampa came home from the war changed and tense. Even as a small child, I could sense that some of the old joy between them had left and was not coming back. Part of him was the same, but part of him was a stranger, less connected to us than his dark memories. From conversations growing up, I had learned that Grampa, my papa, was on a ship during the war; he never really said much about it. My momma knew his pals got that part of him that she wasn't given. She made me promise before she died that, even with his temper, I must look after him in his old age. I must admit, your father had more patience with Grampa than I did." Sophia hesitated, her eyes welling just noticeably. "Miko, just remember that your grandfather Demetrius did the best he could, and he loved you in his own way."

Miko sat speechless as Sophia blotted the moist corners of her eyes with her apron. Her perfunctory words seemed to give her solace in the saying, as though they had long been held back for the right time. She rose slowly and picked up pace as there may be more solace gained from busying herself anew with kitchen tasks.

"Anyway, Miko," Sophia deflected, her soft tone and composure restored, "dreams are crazy, and most don't mean a thing. Put your writing away. If it is meant to be, you will come back to it. And if you ever discover any truths about such things before I am gone, maybe you can help me understand." Patting her already dry hands on the apron, she turned back to Miko with her trademark inverted, skeptical smile. "And I'm not going anywhere for a very long time!"

CHAPTER 1
WATCH YOUR BACK

The fisherman's life Kostas loved was not an easy one. During the years when Miko had been in medical school, Kostas's pride and joy for his son was distracted by the turmoil in the fishing business, not just around Salamina, but the whole Mediterranean. The catches were still generally good, yet the bigger, outside world was kicking the fishermen in many ways. A downturn in the global economy made prices suffer. Pay to crewmen had stagnated, creating a migrant labor force. It was hard to keep fit men, young or old, on the job for long. In that spiral, the contagion of the drug trade had spread to Vathi and surroundings. Fishing boats had been commandeered to obscure shipments along the coast. Those vessels with smaller crews seemed to be targeted more. New hires were scrutinized brutally as the word ran round that some job-seekers may only sign-on to flag targets for the kingpins. Most captains had begun finding and bringing their own firearms aboard. The fishermen at Vathi Village shared the news each had gathered, no one knowing quite what stories to believe. A sense of siege laid in, and fear spread that greater violence would erupt into open conflict between the runners and the fish trade. Any help from the Hellenic Coast Guard always seemed a bit slow and anemic in its response, leaving suspicions that some of its crews were part of a clandestine arrangement.

At the close of workdays, Kostas felt his own draining anxiousness to reach the harbor again and secure his vessel as best he could. Between paying out his two recent crewmen at the end of each week and wondering if they would show again on Mondays, he longed to have an ally like a son at his side yet never mentioned such ideas to Sophia or anyone else lest word get to Miko. Kostas's thin comfort was that his son had escaped this nastiness spoiling everything. At considerable shame to Kostas, Miko's would-be success as a doctor may be a lifeline to which his parents may turn to get by if it comes to that. In the meantime, Kostas would do as other fishermen; he carried the pistol that Demetrius had long ago squirreled away through obscure means. The longer hugs from Sophia before leaving to work in the mornings belied their shared preoccupation. They would not dwell on the troubles openly, so as not to give fear any more power over them.

"Kostas, can you hear me alright?" Sophia scoffed at the breaking-up of their voices she blamed on the cheapness of Kostas's flip-phone cellular he still had in 2016. The engine's drone was not helping. "Should we switch to the radio?"

Kostas had pulled the engine to idle. "No. Is that better?"

"Yes, much better. I can hear you now. If you can get there by three, the doctor wants you to come in to go over that scan of your back today. Is that getting any better?"

"I don't know. No, it's about the same. I can probably make it by three. Let them know. It bothers me more when it's quiet at night than when I'm working. I don't really see it slowing me down today. But, yes, I'll go in and see what she has to say."

Sophia's eye rolling was a reflex each time she heard one of the fishermen complain of his back pain. Among them, the complaining seemed to be competitive, she mused. She and Kostas agreed to get him checked out since his sleep had gotten rough. Even with a good appetite, the food he had been leaving on the table was beginning to show in his face. Before Miko went to university, now nearing the six years' end, the two males in the house had never left a crumb between them.

Ψ

"Mr. Papagiannis, good to see you again. How are you feeling today?"

"You tell me, Doctor! I'll feel better if you tell me I've earned an early medical pension, ha-ha! The back ache is about the same; I'm still getting the work done."

"Yes, well, the CAT scan you got on Thursday shows something of concern. Let me explain. Oh, is your wife in the waiting area? Anyway, let me explain to you first."

Kostas was still amused by his own attempt at humor and hadn't heard anything before the 'let me explain.' "Yes, go on, doctor, I'm sorry for interrupting."

"Your back pain is probably from a bone in the middle part of the spine that looks like it has been partly crushed, kind of like a beer can. Okay? There also seems to be a bit of erosion on the front side of it. We asked for a scan to look at the bones, but there is also something unusual in the soft tissues in front of the bone, and that may be what is damaging the bone. We need to look further into this. I'm going to arrange for some blood work and other tests. At each step, we'll tell you what to expect and how it will help us get to the answer. You should ask Sophia to come with you for visits for now, so we are all sharing the same information."

"Okay. You sound like this is something serious." Kostas's voice dropped. He wasn't ready to ask anything else yet.

"You should know me by now, Kostas," sounding more personal than the fisherman was accustomed to at his infrequent visits to the clinic. "I'm always serious until I'm sure you are well, and we are not there until I get more information. But we'll always be here to answer your questions as best we can. Do you think you need anything for the pain?"

CHAPTER 2
THE RAPTURE

Married now to an accountant of the same frugal mindset, Miko's road to riches would include a bit of miserliness now—avoiding debt, grabbing side income streams where they could, and capitalizing their future earning potential. Bia's earning power might suffer for now, but the investment in Miko's professional training in the States would surpass the relative losses. The time in America would be worth it. In many smaller ways, they had convinced each other through creative and specious ruminations that what they felt like doing was the right thing to do. Each loved the other the more for such games. The dungeon, as they referred to their basement apartment in one of the few gentrified homes near Tulsa's city center, fit this model in price, as did the walking distance to their jobs. Splashing out was when Bia would take a bus or their used Corolla to the suburbs to shop in decentralized Americana.

Miko stared at the light penetrating the dungeon's two small rectangular windows just above head level, lacking a view of the world except for the feet and ankles of an occasional passerby. Even that was often obscured by one of the galvanized steel garbage cans accommodating the multi-unit rental conversion. Bia worried more than Miko did about his doldrums when he would drift into a nearly motionless state, like a sailboat in irons. No obvious stress or harm, the quiet mood meant there was no wind in these moments to move him forward. Fortunately, she had found these stalls did not last long, nor did the free-floating edginess that would follow. She had seen him buffeted before.

Lykeio, the grades when students began their self-division into humanities or science and technology tracks in their education, relied on an often-premature determination of self and destiny. When they met in the last year of *lykeio*, Miko had revealed to Bia his disillusionment with his own lack-luster performance in creative writing during these formative years. His primary school teachers had pointed to his ability to write with the elegance of a prodigy. Miko and his parents had bought into the irony. Now, even in his deepest moments, the muse that had toyed with him had withered, and could not be resurrected.

He would dwell on how wrong he had been not to pursue the technical pathway in the first place. Hadn't it been obvious by the time he was fifteen? Working with his father on the fishing boat on early mornings and weekends, he had shown a level of wizardry toward anything mechanical, from aging and newer engines that mobilized the Vathi fishing fleets to their radios and navigational kit. He had often demonstrated better judgment in the secure transfer of vessels from mooring to dry dock than many older men who had swung the cranes for decades.

Early in his university medical curriculum, a human physiology course had convinced Miko that his ambivalence had all been testosterone-based. He hadn't been able to shed a tear over anything since he was fourteen, about the time when the urgency to write had emptied like a leaking balloon. Emotive phrasing didn't count as much as solving the practical things that needed to be sorted out. When he was in irons like this, Bia didn't buy any of that. An empty place lingered in him, unresolved, insight denied to both. Any assuaging hypothesis would do for now.

"Don't sweat it, Bia," Miko would say. "It's the lucky few who have had a straight line from their first aspirations to what they finally end up doing in school or as a profession. I'm lucky to be here."

"I know, baby," Bia would soothe. "And maybe someday you will try writing again when you have free time."

Mischief in Miko's grin and eyes signaled his emergence from the funk. "When I was little, I thought I would write things to touch people's souls, not so much their minds, bodies, or pocketbooks. But, if I must be boring to do some good . . .," Miko bolted from his chair and swept Bia up from behind with both arms doubled around her slender waist. He swirled her about the tiny room with her legs flying over the low furniture. "Then it will be your job to make sure that I do not become entirely boring!"

"Ha, right—boring!" Bia chided. "I am still finding pieces of your puzzle. So, behave, now! Let me cook you some lamb souvlaki tonight. We'll drink a bottle of wine, and you can tell me some stories from your childhood. How's that?"

"May Zeus and the gods be praised! You know my weak spots, Pudding, but I don't know what you expect to get out of me," Miko remarked sheepishly, with more physical outcomes in mind. "But, okay, I'll try to keep you entertained as long as the wine flows." He would once again let Bia's intoxicating effects take hold and seduce him to near lunacy. The basement apartment arrangement considered infernal by others had rather imprinted on him as their den of carnal heaven.

The sequence of events would be unalterable as if defined by the emergence of springtime. The finicky old-school radiator gradually mitigated the otherwise perpetual chill in the dungeon, kept crisp by the concrete walls. Pungent smells of merging olive oil and spices gently burnt, varying bursts of vegetable and lamb aromas, each became another siren to be resisted. Then would come Bia's soft, melodious humming of some new American tune that she had not quite mastered, a sign of her growing satisfaction with the outcome of the culinary process. Miko would imagine holograms of her mother, grandmother, and one or more aunts around her, lifting a brow and nodding and whispering tacit approval. Bia's soft, wordless cooing signaled the approaching culmination of the process and the moment at which Miko's eyes must depart the computer screen for the evening, lest he miss her unconscious hip-swaying to her own lost melody. Her motion evoked all his appetites, shifting instincts from cognitive to primal function. It was time to set the table for an evening of real life with the brain removed. Sight, smell, salivation, and Pavlovian gastric responses led; an Argentine Malbec indistinguishable from the wines from the hillsides of home would complete the indulgence. Smiles and eye contact obviated words between the young couple, enjoying the life they had created together, the hard study and self-discipline taken in stride.

"Had you ever hoped for simple and fulfilling days like this, Bia?"

"You know, we plan and plan for some kind of success, not knowing that success happens in these moments." Bia paused. "I love you, Miko, and I love these moments. Let me die quickly in one of them, so that I will not know I've passed for a long time."

Retreating to the makeshift "living room/bedroom," dishes left on the kitchen table, Bia settled her shoulders deep into the corner of the worn, rented couch and tilted her head, eyes and soft mouth widened in anticipation. Miko replied with his unfettered boyish grin.

"Okay, one story," Miko began. He dramatized with a slack jaw and empty eyes, swallowed hard, and without her permission, commandeered the dregs of her Malbec into his own near-empty glass and ignoring her gratuitous punch to his shoulder. A random choice from his many childhood stories, Miko took pains to recreate for her the day long ago when he and Kostas had watched the *Nearchos* shelled and sunk off St. Georgios Island, the curious dream that followed, and the veritable compulsion he had felt to write it down. When he finished, his wandering eyes focused back on hers, where he detected naught but somnolence.

"Really?" Bia feigned a yawn.

"Okay, make fun of me after you asked for this!" Miko protested, already throwing off the cushions and beginning to unfold the sofa bed with her still upright, and brows lifted coyly. "For this, you will pay dearly!"

CHAPTER 3
THE ADMISSION

Miko found it uncanny how often his pager would go off just as sleep was becoming real, presumably at the crossover from stage three to stage four non-REM. Tightness at the temples would follow the brief wave of nausea and reflux. He would lie still, knowing it would pass quickly as consciousness resumes; drawing a few deep breaths helped. This time, at least, the pager didn't signal a code blue or someone trying to die on one ward or another; no running would be involved. Probably an admission, a process typically involving the conduction of a complete history and physical and composing a ranked problem list. An admission constitutes the acceptance of the person into the hospital, wholesale, for complete care by professionals, setting into motion orders for testing and treatment based upon what was knowable at the time. The Tulsa County Public Health Hospital also served as the regional Veterans Administration and Indian Health inpatient repositories, and god-forbid, for any merchant marine folk passing along with the minuscule volume of shipping on the Arkansas River.

Miko remembered it was Saturday night, or now early Sunday morning, when all the drunks across the city of Tulsa would aggregate for the knife-and-gun club activities, in the parlance of the medical and surgical residents manning the emergency departments and surgical suites on the weekends. Muggy days of June, when the moon was full, would typically be an auspicious time for a bit of rage and bloodletting. Two in the morning was the classic hour in the interns' long shift when the normal world turned upside-down. Why not, he thought. He had just finished Emergency Room back-up at 1:00 a.m.

"Dr. Papagiannis here. What have you got for me?" To the staff, Miko seemed more articulate than most, even if it was his second language, and maybe because it was his second language.

"Dr. Pajamas. Well good! Hey sweetie!" The booming voice left no question as to the identity of Maggie, the black night nursing supervisor on the neurology ward, Three South. She was the one who had given him hell as a new arrival last July when his clinical skills were near non-existent, let alone an appreciation for what he had gotten himself into. Now it was a relief to hear her voice, a joy in fact, so much was his gratitude, and every other intern's gratitude for that matter, for her effective tutelage. Her demands on the interns to move their asses getting things done in a timely fashion had been matched by her personal dedication to helping them find their asses when it came to mastery of the practical art of IVs, venipunctures, the slippage of catheters into any available body orifice in need of one. She had a knack of weaving in some endearing mispronunciation of names that ironically made her the unforgettable one. She had become an institution within the institution, at least on the graveyard shift. Future patients of those blooming physicians would have neither a concept nor an appreciation of the invisible Maggies who had dragged their ultimately competent, godlike doctors over a critical threshold of maturation at some sick house in the dread of dark nights.

"We have one of your favorites to admit. The ER has blessed you with a drunk and disorderly white male veteran that Tulsa's finest dropped off. Says the cops were unsure if they saw seizure activity or not, so that bought him a room with us for observation. He also had a handgun on him, with only one bullet, apparently, and said they didn't know if he was planning to use it on himself or some other genius."

"Yes, Miss Magpie. Hell, why not? See you shortly." Running one hand through his hair as he slipped his feet one by one into his Crocs, he drew two more deep breaths before rocking to a standing position. He delayed the whack of turning on the light until he could wash his face. Self-care was an important part of internship survival. And he had now almost completed the required rotating post-graduate year one—his last night of in-house call as the final days of this inglorious phase ticked by. He was buoyed by the thought of crossing that crucial line, almost smiling. They can't hurt me anymore now, he thought, whatever the rest of this god-forsaken night brings. Draping the stethoscope around his neck, he stuffed the sign-out notes, pen, and pen-light back into his scrub shirt pocket, adjusted the scrub bottoms that had shifted so far to the right in his brief, tortured snooze that he was sporting a skewed wedgie.

The walls of the empty ward, now seconding as sleeping rooms for the on-call house staff, echoed each footstep despite his best efforts to be discrete, if perchance, any of his kind were indeed enjoying the opportunity for a moment of shut-eye. Miko marveled at how those who had found their calling in obstetrics didn't seem to mind the night shift up-and-down so much, whereas the anesthesia residents were the world's worst whiners about being awakened to put someone to sleep.

The ironies played out in thought as he approached the occupied wards, shrugging neck and shoulders. He would make a point to remember this night in symbolism. Passage from medical internship to psychiatry residency was eminent, both training phases counting the year from July through June. Residency kept the fledgling doctors mostly within the walls of the inpatient and outpatient domains of a hospital whose medical staff would guide their training. Miko had already finished an incredibly more humane post-graduate year one in Greece, simultaneously struggling through the grueling testing process for foreign trainees seeking to matriculate in coveted US residency programs.

Nearing the Three South patient ward, he imagined his last such admission would be drawn from the usual menu: (a) real disease, hopefully an untreated seizure disorder, even if the most apparent cause was alcohol-related; (b) the alcoholism itself—dealing with the slow self-destruction of substance abuse, the aspect of medicine, even psychiatry, for which he had a meager appetite, and (c) suicidal ideation and planning, i.e., the "cry for help" of major depression masked by the drinking. Not a bad raffle, if you are into bread-and-butter psychopathology. Not as fascinating as schizophrenia, but this would be the foundation for many a suburban psychiatrist. Miko saw his future in that world, as opposed to this institutional stuff.

"Mr. Connolly's chart is in the rack, Doctor—327B, unless the aide is getting vitals again," broadcast the ward clerk as Miko arrived. "The other five beds in the suite are empty, so Maggie put him in there not knowing how rowdy he will get. Maggie wanted me to tell you the police left him with a single wrist shackled to the bed until he's cleared about the gun he had. But he's just sleeping. No other restraints. Rails down. ED ordered a phenytoin and Librium protocol for the night."

Miko nodded appreciatively and quickly checked the handwritten ED notes, vitals, med list, and orders. The two-drug protocol would offset the potential for withdrawal seizures and would also make it a further challenge to get information in the resulting state of sedation.

Maggie poked a head out of the med room, taking care not to lose her count in the reconciliation process. "Dr. P, are sure you want to go into psych? You know, you're doing damn good now as a real doctor."

"You never miss a chance, do you, Miss Magpie?" Shaking his head, Miko grinned and turned, and was quickly absorbed in the shadows of the spare night-shift ambiance.

Semi-prone and snoring, Miko's patient was still in street clothes except for shoes, oblivious to the light and the single handcuff securing his right wrist to the bar at the head of the bed. Miko knew how this would go. His job was to process the admission thoroughly regardless of the hour and impediments, documenting all in cogent medicalese. Ordinarily, the whole process would take him less than an hour. This fellow, and so many like him who had graced his call nights before, was narcotized already, just wanted to sleep, did not consider himself sick, and would need reminding of his present whereabouts repeatedly. The positive side was that the fight was out of him by now, as opposed to the police work and the ED staff confrontation that had surely preceded this peaceful encounter in the abyss of the night. Miko gently touched the back of his patient's shoulder to minimize the risk of startle.

"Mr. Connolly? Can you hear me? I'm Dr. Papagiannis. I need to ask you some questions and then do a brief exam."

The head raised slowly, eyes squinting unevenly against the light that peered over Dr. Papagiannis' shoulder. "Um, okay," The patient muttered with a straining, dry mouth.

"Can you tell me what brought you to the hospital tonight?" Miko started, noting the snoring had already resumed. Miko looked around, confirming they were alone, reached out from his chair and silently drew the door closed. Sitting again comfortably in his chair, Miko raised his right foot and, with a kick of his heel, rattled the entire metal cage-framed bed. "Mr. Connolly, are you having any pain anywhere?"

The kicks to the bed would follow with regularity, and with each, one or two questions and answers might be exchanged over the next 20-30 seconds before somnolence takes the patient back. Most queries would be answered in the negative for convenience and, alas, the faster pathway back to sleep. Less cooperation was needed for the physical exam; indeed, even in a coma, one can be relatively confident by way of the five senses that the patient is stable and medically safe under observation.

"Okay, Mr. Connolly. We've ordered some medicine to help you with the withdrawal process and help keep you calm." Miko wrapped up. "Is there anything you need right now?" he asked the sleeping man. "In that case, I'll see you again in the morning."

The sleeping man would have little or no recollection of the encounter, tomorrow or ever. Pretty routine, thank god, Miko thought. The admission proceeded as inauspiciously as with most of the myriad forgotten souls Miko had cared for here, except for the dubious 'last call' distinction of this oblivious character. Miko scribbled out diet and observational orders, urine drug screen, chemistries and cell count, flagged the chart for the ward clerk, and glanced quickly at his digital watch—4:13 a.m. Damn, he thought, not bad! If he can get some shut-eye until 6:45 a.m., he could get to sign out, make rounds, and be out by 11:00 a.m., leaving a bit of Sunday for real life.

CHAPTER 4
201 STATUS

Miko caught up with the junior medical resident being swarmed by a gaggle of scrubs whose night had been even busier than Miko's. Most of the bedraggled interns were mentally out the door already, approaching the end of a brutal shift.

"I'm just going to have you interns present your admissions briefly in the hallway," the ranking resident announced. "Unless it's critical, the only others I want to hear about are any discharges you expect today." In the rundown of admissions and discharges, a couple of exceptions caught the resident's attention for potential teaching moments. Miko's 2:00 a.m. hit was one of them.

In a sequence by room number, the entourage found Miko's patient just before 9:00 a.m., still shackled, alone in the six-bed ward. Yawning his disinterest as the group corralled, he dabbled over dry toast, applesauce, and black coffee, his reintroduction to more complex calorie sources. As Miko cleared his throat to begin, the day shift charge nurse stuck his head in the door.

"Sorry, team. Dr. P, admitting is calling to clarify the status. Is Mr. Connolly 201 or 302?" the nurse asked in a hushed voice. The coding shorthand kept the passage of such information brief and obscure. "ED didn't specify."

"Stand by, Dave; I'll let you know in a few minutes." Miko proceeded. "Good morning, Mr. Connolly. Again, I'm Dr. Papagiannis. We met last night when you came in. You may not remember much about that."

"Pretty sleepy then. No, not much. Nice to see you again, anyway. Not many people call me Mr. Connolly," the disheveled patient mumbled with a half grin, giving a quick glance and nod to each of the other faces. "Y'all can just call me AJ."

"Well, these are my colleagues. I've briefly explained to them the circumstances that brought you to the hospital last night. How are you doing this morning?"

"Probably not worth a shit," AJ chuckled. "No worries, I'll be out of here after I finish this."

Standing behind AJ across the bed from Miko, the ranking resident gave a silent nod toward the door, obsequiously providing his snap judgment that there was nil to learn from this chap on a Sunday morning after all.

"Well, since you're still eating, let's let the group move on, but there's something I need to ask you, Mr. Connolly, in private." Miko opened the door a bit wider as the others shuffled out. "I'll catch up . . . ," he called to senior resident.

"What are the numbers about, the 201 or whatever?" the patient asked, brushing the crumbs from his hands, before sniffing the coffee. "This joe is actually pretty good."

Miko found the patient's capture of the fleeting conversation with the charge nurse curious. "Ah, well, basically, it's a medical coding thing, whether you are admitted voluntarily, a 201, or if you are our guest on a non-voluntary basis."

Miko gently settled on the bedside, organizing the sensitive question. "Last night the police brought you to the hospital in a state of intoxication. The report was that you were found a bit incoherent. As they were putting you in the squad car, they confiscated a weapon from you. So here's the situation. The reason you are handcuffed to the bed is that this is a non-voluntary admission, a 302, until there is time to evaluate whether you are a potential harm to yourself or others. So we can't let you leave today. As a matter of fact, until you are considered medically stable and we can move you to a locked psychiatry ward for observation and treatment, the shackle will have to remain."

"Is that so?" AJ replied compliantly. "So am I under arrest, or what?"

"Not really, but yes, effectively. You'll be with us for at least forty-eight hours. Then, depending on your assessment, we'll figure out how long you have to stay."

"Assessment?" AJ asked, more engaged now, with the rest of the entourage departed. "Of what?"

"Well, to be frank, why you had the gun. If you were thinking of harming yourself, it means something different from if you meant to harm someone else. That determination will help guide how long you stay and where you go from here. You are a veteran, so if you chose to stay for evaluation and management on your own after forty-eight hours, then we can decide together how long that will be. And perhaps the authorities won't be involved any longer. You don't have to decide that right now, but you can't go home today."

"Home," AJ echoed, his stare frozen on the white ceramic coffee cup. He sighed deeply and rubbed his eyes. He studied Miko's face for a moment, making his own assessment, and looked back to the cup. "Yeah, maybe I need to stay a bit."

Ψ

Miko was the first of the new psychiatry training cohort to arrive for the orientation meeting on July first, barely three days past his last night of ward duty as an intern. He felt rested enough now and arrived early to assuage the first-day butterflies. The conference room within the administrative suite of the psychiatry department at Public Health was unique for its generous bay window, a vestige of a previous half-turret on the river side of the stately art deco structure. From the sixth-floor perch, his gaze followed a long, flat barge as it wound its way cautiously along the Arkansas River, barely navigable through the west margin of the city. Distracting thoughts of engine size, draft, weight distribution, and ordinary things calmed Miko. The department secretary fussed with the overhead PowerPoint projection, breaking to welcome other arrivals to waiting seats, where they traded quiet introductions. Some had arrived from other hospital programs. Miko drew a deep breath and moved to join them. The secretary called the meeting to order from the dignified wooden podium bearing the Greek letter Psi, ψ, a universal symbol for study and care of the mind, similarly etched on the frosted pane of the department door. Miko could go on about how much of Western medicine had deep roots in his homeland; no one had ever asked. The secretary introduced the chief of psychiatry who gently shooed her away from behind when she started reading his bio. Miko was underwhelmed by the caricature of a stodgy, aged physician who may be fighting the end of an unremarkable career—until the chief started speaking.

"The Diagnostic and Statistical Manual, in the 1978 version we called DSM-3, and through its updates since then, I think most of us would agree, represented a great leap forward in the objectivity of psychiatric diagnosis," the chief of service began. "It is a far more evidence-based guide than we'd had previously. More than ever before, these efficient compendia aligned psychiatric practice with modern, western, evidence-based medical approach in general. We left the theory-based realm of suspicion and innuendo, and sharpened the boundaries of what constitutes illness, variance, and conditioning. You, sitting before me, are stepping into this field already better equipped than practitioners and psychologists who, only a generation before you, would have spent an entire career accumulating enough experience to distill but a fraction of the depth and clarity available to you in the current compilation of the manual. Use it diligently."

The chief paused and moved away from the podium toward the bay window. A vista of a blue sky, sporting billows of flat-bottomed cumulus clouds immediately refocused the eyes and consciousness of all in the room tracking his motion. Miko sensed this was not a random stroll by the chief but perfectly timed to draw the new residents into another thought dimension.

"We are not our minds," the chief began anew, "but how we live in the mind almost solely determines our experience of the world and our satisfaction with it. Together with the breathtaking pace of advancement in behavioral and pharmacological therapies constantly expanding our armamentarium, yours will be a rich and rewarding career, as you continue to push the boundaries outward. Never underestimate the adventure your patients will lead you to in their infinite individuality. And never forget that it is a human being that you are tagging with a diagnosis, however accurate or vague. Never forget the power inherent in your skill at showing the patient a mirror unto him- or herself, with kindness rather than the emotional or physical violence the rest of the world reflects upon them. Remain curious and nonjudgmental, and not only will you accomplish a great deal of good, but your patients will mold you to be the best version of who you are meant to be. Welcome to the program! Under my watch, this institution will do its best to prepare you, and what I ask in return is that you give its patients the best you have."

Miko felt himself shrink into his chair as he peered about at the other half-dozen new junior psychiatry residents, taking measure of their reactions. He had expected the elder chief of service to be remote, especially to the foreign medical graduates who were over-represented in US psychiatry programs. How could the chief make these profound and penetrating comments off the cuff—no notes or slides. Miko's contemporaries appeared equally spell-bound. The ethical nobility of new physicians can be eroded during the grinding process of training; Miko figured the chief's rhetoric was intended to put his protégées at a higher starting point.

The formal orientation lasted all of thirty minutes, mostly consisting of distribution of the clinic patients being turned over from the finishing cohort, a few policy statements, the inpatient ward assignments, and, of course, the call schedule.

The durability of the metal desks and chairs in the ambulatory psychiatry clinic was self-evident. Like remnants of the structure's early architecture, they formed parts of an austere museum chic. A new desk blotter restored some youth to the spare spaces within a government budget. Miko took a two-inch square analogue timepiece out of its box and placed it facing him on the corner of the desk, obscured from patients by an in/out box. He would always know the time without patients catching him ogling his watch.

By 2:00 p.m., Miko had already finished visits with three legacy follow-up patients turned over from some happy residency grad. He took some comfort that his prior post-graduate year in Athens, however less intense, and the gen med internship just concluded were already making a difference. Those rotations had given him just enough exposure to the commonly administered anti-depressants and anti-psychotics, as well as their common adverse effects and drug interactions, that he would navigate less anemically through the first day. He had already jotted down a dozen questions to look up this evening. Between patients, Miko peered out the tall office window toward the parking lot and grassy areas below the sixth-floor perch. He felt a wave of good fortune flow over. He had arrived. He would devour this learning. He would come to know a trade that nurtures the mind and soul, as his father's commercial fishing nurtured the muscle of communities. He would come to know himself and meet whatever doubts dwelled within.

Miko peered into the hallway where patients sat in rows of chairs along the walls. Using a single room each, the residents fetched their own patients from this holding arrangement, consistently reminded by the clinic nursing staff that no bottlenecks would be tolerated. His printed schedule indicated the next patient was new to the psychiatry clinic. Miko highlighted the name with a bit of ceremony, mentally marking this as his own first official new psychiatry patient.

"AJ Connolly?" Miko called. He made eye contact with a man who rose quickly from about twenty seats away and began his approach. The name was familiar, but the appearance less so.

"Please have a seat, Mr., uh, Connolly. I'm Dr. Miko Papagiannis, a psychiatry resident."

AJ squinted at the name tag on Miko's lab jacket. "Yes. We've met—when I first came in a few nights ago, and then again, the next morning. I may be confused. You young folks all look alike to me." AJ smiled. "It sounds like the same accent I remember. You were a regular doctor then. Are you a psychiatrist now?"

"Ah, that's right. I remember now. We can both be excused—our first meeting was in the middle of the night, and sometimes that can seem like a distant dream, right?" Miko kept the irony to himself, that his last patient of gen med night call was now his first new psychiatry patient. "Let's see, that was three or four days ago. You're still here and now referred to the mental health ambulatory clinic. And, yes, I'm now training in psychiatry, which will be my long-term specialty. So, good! Let's catch up. What has been happening with you since then?"

"Well, mainly just tests these last few days. With my history of a bypass and valve replacement, I've had x-rays and an echocardiogram, and some ultrasounds on my legs and so forth. I used to smoke, so they sent me for a breathing test. Bunch of stuff like that . . ."

"What do you know about the results." Miko scanned the clinical notes for complications observed since the admission. "They are not all charted yet. Any mentions by your other doctors?"

"Everything's good, except the breathing test results are not back yet. I suspect that's pretty good too, since I'm still breathing." AJ joked.

"Has it been explained to you why you were referred to psychiatry?" Miko tactfully probed the patient's assimilation of information since first meeting the inebriated man whose bed he had kicked repeatedly to just get through the admission formalities.

"Well, you said that I'd be 'assessed' as you called it. I guess I'm here to be assessed."

"Yes, that's right, Mr. Connolly," Miko confirmed.

"I think I've probably said it six or seven times since I've been in this joint; you can dispense with the Mr. Connolly crap—just call me AJ. And I'll call you Miko if you don't mind. I could fuck up Papa-whatever more ways than Sunday, if you know what I mean." AJ was surprised at his own unnecessary crudeness, a fallback when he felt nervous.

"No worries, of course," Miko assented, "we can have a proper doctor-patient relationship without formal titles, if you are comfortable with that."

AJ nodded agreement.

"Okay, let's start from the beginning." Miko rolled out the context of the admission notes. "The police found you in a semi-conscious state and moved to have you checked out medically in the ER. Ordinarily, then, they might just take you home to sleep it off. In your case, however, there's the matter of the pistol they found on you. So they brought you here for involuntary admission," Miko slowed down, noting AJ's furrowed brow and tilted head. "Which means we get involved, first to make sure you are medically stable, and then we sort out the underlying issues of potential violence from both the legal and mental health viewpoints. Does that make sense?"

"Sure. No problem." AJ looked around the spare office, tucking his hands into his jacket pockets, zipped up against the chill lingering from his alcohol abstinence within the drafty edifice. "It's good that someone dragged my sorry ass off the street. Sorry for all the hassle. It's not really like me to create a stink."

"There's an entry on the admitting police report that your only prior arrest was twenty years ago, again for carrying a loaded weapon, and you were released after an overnight stay in city hall, without prosecution" Miko probed. "Is that about it?"

AJ nodded. "That's about it."

"And how are you feeling today, AJ? Are you still thinking about harming someone?" Miko's tone was direct, yet non-confrontational.

"No," AJ responded hesitantly. "But it does crop up from time to time. I start drinking to calm myself down, but it can backfire. Some little thing—a comment somebody makes might set me off. I'm tired of this, over and over. I gotta figure it out."

"Help me understand why you were armed that night. The police record indicates that there was one bullet in the pistol's chamber. What can you tell me about that, AJ?" Miko continued general questions led by factual observations, and just enough experience to anticipate where he might get pushback.

"Can I be frank with you, Doc?"

"That's what we're here for, AJ." Miko affirmed with open arms.

"I've managed to hurt the people I love the most. I've got to change, or I need to just end it. But it seems I'm too big a coward to do that." AJ snickered.

"AJ, it seems that you have come to a crossroads." Miko reframed. "Let's talk about what brought you here. Have you been feeling depressed?"

"Sometimes, a little, I guess. You know, it may sound funny, but that night, I didn't feel depressed. Yeah, I got plastered, but I didn't feel depressed. It was like it all came clear to me. You're right, I arrived at the crossroads. I didn't like me as I am. And I wasn't sure what would make me feel better—shooting me or somebody who needed it more. That may sound simpleminded and a bit lame."

"Listen AJ, for today, we've got about, uh, about twenty minutes more. So how about if I just shut up, and you tell me about how you got to this crossroads. And if we need more time, we'll have it in the coming weeks. How does that sound? Okay?" Miko would consciously fake it until he could make it. Until he learned some real psychoanalysis, he would draw on the bits of second-year medical school behavioral psychology that stuck. There had been an exam question regarding junctions in self-realization that can be exploited in the transition to insights and the therapeutic mode. He had gotten the test answer wrong, he recalled, and which is probably why he remembered it now.

AJ looked up at the large white-faced clock high on the wall above the door. He had installed probably a hundred such clocks at St. Francis Hospital, the premier tidy, well-equipped, full-service, private hospital on Tulsa's wealthy south side where he worked. The second hand trembled with each precise, impatient kick forward, demanding, until he could almost feel it in his chest.

"Where do I start? I'm sick of me. I'm guilty of making my wife's life miserable. She has endured a lot of punishment, and she doesn't deserve any of it. I can't make up for it. She'd be better off without me," AJ reaffirmed.

"Wow," Miko aimed to puncture the self-loathing as a barrier to therapy. "You really sound like a rotten guy! Have you always been such a creep?"

AJ took the bait and grinned at the novice. "Not really. But there are some things that get stuck in my craw that I could probably find better ways to deal with."

"So, with the time left today, why don't you tell me about the alcohol? When did you start drinking?" Miko would plow through the easy-peasy stuff every medical student should know to ask and document.

"I suppose that started in the Navy. I joined up when I was seventeen, just as we were getting into Vietnam. Sure, I had had a few beers in high school. In the Navy, you know, everybody drinks in port, so that's when it got to be sort of routine. Nobody thinks anything of it," AJ minimized.

"Family history of alcoholism?" Miko assembled the usual risk factors in his note-taking.

AJ paused. "Not really, except, well, my younger brother Mike was in for detox once and then rehab to keep his job."

Have there been any effects on your own work life because of your drinking? Ever been fired or disciplined because of missed work or tardiness—anything related to drinking?"

"No. I didn't let it. I couldn't let it," AJ defended. "See, I'm an electrician, and you can't be impaired in the least bit when working with electricity. You might get yourself fried. And that's not good! Anyway, I guess I just like to drink, Doc," AJ admitted, ". . . probably too much. I don't know if that's really my problem. Sailors are famous for drinking, maybe, but most are probably not all fucked up like me. It certainly hasn't helped."

Miko skimmed the lab and imaging results in the chart as he listened. "What medical problems have you encountered because of alcohol that you are aware of?"

AJ scratched his forehead. "Well, I've had a heart bypass and a valve replacement, but that's probably mostly related to past smoking, or so I've been told."

"You mentioned problems with your wife. I want to come back to that since it seems to be key to, let's say, your discouragement. Maybe there's something to unpack there. Would you be willing to go into those things?" Miko probed gingerly for the open versus more sensitive areas for discussion, hoping his inexperience would not be too obvious. "Were there experiences during your military service that you've had trouble dealing with? Often, veterans carry burdens from those combat experiences or the military environment in general."

"Whatever you want to ask me is okay. But it's probably not what you think. I actually enjoyed my time in the Navy. People who have been in the service, particularly combat vets, understand how it is. Some deal with it better than others."

"Well, thank you for that, AJ." Miko was becoming more conscious of the time. Running behind in clinic puts everyone off—patients, staff, and housekeeping—reality annoyingly gets a vote in therapy, he thought. He lingered momentarily, looking to pause the conversation, and wind up the session. "So let's do this. Let me see you back in clinic in two days' time. We'll talk again, then. I'd like you to think about it and come back prepared to tell me about your relationship with your wife, and about your military time. Are you okay with that?"

"Okay, but most people don't really want to hear the service time—not even my family. It's just not in their wheelhouse."

Miko hoped a personal disclosure would help in creating common ground. "You know, AJ, I had a grandfather in the Royal Greek Navy in WWII, and even as a boy, I had a sense that it had taken a toll on him. I've never been in the military myself, so I can assure you that I have no personal point of reference to make judgments about what you may have experienced or how those experiences may affect people. Maybe we'll learn something from each other."

"Yeah, we'll see." AJ chuckled. "Don't expect much."

"Before you go," Miko remembered, as AJ rose a bit stiffly to leave, "I'm going to give you this contract to read and think about. It is an agreement that you will continue to follow up with us here in the clinic on a regular schedule for therapy, and that you will contact the hospital immediately if you're in trouble and thinking again about harming yourself. We can talk about the contract when you come back and about us both signing it before you are discharged. Okay?"

"Okay. By the way, a sheriff's deputy stopped by my room yesterday morning saying that based on the hospital's report, the district attorney is still deciding whether to issue a warrant on me for illegal carry and public disorder. Is there anything you can do about that? I'd sure like to not have that hanging over my head."

"That's a good question, AJ." Miko would bob and weave, having no idea, yet, of how these legal matters were managed. "It is my understanding that such matters are handled at the department level in a public institution like this. I'll try to get you an answer. Since no harm came to others from your actions, I suspect the outcome will be favorable."

"You mean I may have dodged a bullet, so to speak?" AJ joked, sheepishly.

Miko grinned back. "Now you're killing me, AJ! Get out of here, already!"

Barely able to stifle a yawn, AJ shuffled out toward the ward. Miko paused from scribbling a note into the paper chart already tagged to be digitized, to observe AJ's movement and balance. Miko regretted not probing how this man of sixty-five was only now encountering the system to address what had probably been a lifetime of issues. There was an odd filament of refinement in this inconspicuous man, who at first blush seemed lost in an odyssey for redemption. Oh, well, this is psychiatry, Miko concluded, even less attractive to patients than dentistry. This was not a seizure, myocardial infarction, or ketoacidosis. The dimensions of the mind would unfold in their own good time, and not by titrating the re-balancing of electrolytes. It already felt familiar. He would hunker down in these two more years and become that best version of himself, as the chief had contended. Then, hopefully, Dr. P would clean up nicely amid the tears of the well-to-do.

CHAPTER 5
OPENING DOORS

AJ arrived at his appointment with Miko well groomed, and looking more rested than two days earlier, sporting a nylon shirt, blue jeans, and penny loafers.

"So how does this generally work?" he asked Miko, who was just settling at the office desk. "You ask me questions and then tell me what to think, and then I'll be alright? In an electrician's work, you trace the circuits, measure current, and map out the solutions. Why can't you geniuses make it that simple?"

Miko was ready. "AJ, my job is more like when you go into a house that you have never seen before. You go into each room and learn what's in there and how it contributes to the life in the house. The rooms are all quite different, but part of the same house. Then you ask what needs to be done in each room to make the whole house a livable home. Can you picture that?"

"I suppose so. So you kind of look at the different parts of someone's life, and see what's not working?"

"Not exactly. You and I will walk through those rooms together and hopefully find the things that are making some rooms uninhabitable. It's less overwhelming that way. Over time, hopefully, one by one, you can put the rooms in order."

"That simple, huh?"

"Not simple at all. But a simple analogy can help the mind keep track of things. Why don't we talk about your marriage first, since that seems to be an area that brings you remorse? Would that be alright with you?"

"Fire away." AJ encouraged.

"How long have you and, uh, it's Natalia, right?" Miko glanced at the chart. "How long have you been married?"

"Forty-seven years." AJ related without coloring one way or another.

"Wow, that may not be a record, but it has to be above average! There's got to be something of value there. Yet you said making her life miserable has been a regret for you. One approach we can take is that you can tell me your view of what your lives together have been like. Then, if she and you agree, I get her side of the story privately, and then we get you together and compare lists of issues. It's not magic, and you won't agree on everything. Maybe you think you don't agree on anything. But sometimes, it's surprising on what you view similarly and what you view differently."

AJ rubbed his chin. "We'd have to see what she says. I don't know if she'd talk to anyone about us."

"Well, at the right time, bring it up and see how she responds to the idea, okay? But for now, we'll focus on just you. It would help me to hear about how you two met and got close. Let's explore that room for a while, if you don't mind."

"Sure," AJ straightened himself in the chair, and cleared his throat. "She must have been thirteen or fourteen when her family moved into the neighborhood. Not long after, when I was about sixteen and started getting interested in girls, all of a sudden, she was the prettiest thing I'd ever seen. Still is. Of course, I didn't know how to behave. I was really, as we say, rough around the edges. Nothing serious happened, because not long after, I signed up for the Navy. I guess I was in love, though. Anyway, we wrote and went back and forth. Eventually, she was the reason I left the Navy when my active duty was up. Otherwise I would have stayed. She could probably remember more for you about our dating, because, well, I probably already had attitude problems even then.

"She dated a friend of mine for some time while I was away. I couldn't blame him, but I got a little nuts for a while thinking I could have lost her by being gone. Anyway, that was over when I finished active duty in four years, and we patched it up.

"When I got home, there were some things that didn't feel right, but I guess I ignored them until it was too late. I had been focused like a laser that I'd get out of the service, get some steady job, I'd somehow buy a house, Natalia and I would get married, we'd start a family, and that would be it—a plan I never had any second thoughts about. It was as if when I was away, the rest of the world would be in suspended animation and just go back to normal when I got out of the service.

"She can fill things in for you from there. I've been selfish and stubborn, and hard on her. Now that the kids are all out, we're just sort of co-existing together and going through the motions. There's a big gap. I don't know if the marriage needs to be over. A lot of interest in life has been slowly squeezed out by living with past mistakes."

"I can tell that you've thought a lot about this, AJ, because you move quickly to potential conclusions," Miko reframed. "At the risk of sounding like a psychiatrist, I'm going to purposely steer you away from conclusions and generalizations until we've had a chance to look into more rooms of your life. Before we finish today, I want to hear something about your own growing up; some stories and background that would help me understand who you are through your own eyes."

"You know, Doc, I have respect for other tradesmen who know their stuff, but not much for phonies. You're a young punk, but you have been straight with me so far, and not just pushing pills. If you think you can fix me up with just talking, I'm in, for now. I appreciate the effort."

"Thanks, AJ. That means a lot to me. We'll take it one room at a time and see what we find." Miko affirmed. "I see in your chart that you reviewed and signed the agreement for follow-up that we talked about last session. I have signed it as well. Our department has authorized clearance for me to discharge you from inpatient status, as early as tomorrow morning, based on this pledge to follow-up with me every two weeks for now, and to alert our call number if you are having urges to harm yourself or others."

"Yes, sir." AJ responded in a regimented fashion, as though a long-latent reflex had been actuated.

"Don't call me sir, I work for a living!" Miko grinned. "I learned that from another vet, an Army sergeant who trained officers to parachute from planes. I love it!"

AJ rolled his eyes.

"Anyway, you'll be happy to know that although you were brought in initially handcuffed, the record will reflect a voluntary admission, and there will not be a record of arrest regarding the reason for admission."

"Hey, I'm good with that, Doc! Thanks!" AJ replied.

"The desk clerk will schedule out your next visits for the initial six weeks and then we'll reassess, okay?" Miko closed the record, motioning toward the door.

CHAPTER 6
FOUNDATIONS

Sweat, pollen, and impatience filled the dog days of Oklahoma August, the only distractions from the bugs. Attempts to keep the aging building climatized for comfort were fraught. Staff would exercise limited options—opening and closing windows throughout the day, deploying box fans for a breeze, fiddling with dubious thermostats and window units in one clinic room or another. Sirens warning of twisters were commonplace in America's tornado alley; staff and clients would gather by protocol in the windowless corridors, all taken in stride.

"Shouldn't I be laying on a couch or something for this review of my whole life." AJ teased.

Miko's blank look morphed into a grimace. "This institution doesn't provide us with couches. Besides, you'd just go to sleep and that would be the end of it, AJ. Just begin where you want to, where you remember feeling you had to fight a lot."

"I have tried to figure out why I react the way I do, both the good and the bad. Around ninth grade, one teacher said I was bitter about something and that made room for meanness. I didn't have any idea what she meant, and didn't care to.

"At that age, I thought had some good characteristics. I wasn't particularly tall, but compact and strong. My old man had shown me some basics of fist fighting—how to guard, throw jabs, hooks and upper cuts, and where to land them. I was on the wrestling team for a while in high school and got cut for smoking, but not before mastering take-downs that fit well with my build. At that age, I always felt ready to fight.

"My other good side was that I was honest, in a way. That is, I tell it like it is and can take being told like it is. I guess I had a short fuse for phonies, show-offs, and bullies. It's occurred to me that that is maybe not the best kind of honesty, since it did lead to more than my share of fights.

"Once, when my younger twin brothers just got into eighth grade, they came home from school one day and told me about a big guy who had been picking on them at school. I told them to tell this guy I'd whip his ass; I'd come to the school, or he could follow them home, made no difference. Well, my god, the dumb shit came to the house—why, I'll never know. In seconds, I had him on the ground and was pounding his head and belly. He was quite a bit bigger than me, but he was just a bully. Bullies are all about intimidation, they never know how to fight. When I let him go, I told him if I ever heard of him picking on anyone, I'd come to their school, walk straight into his class, and beat him up again in front of everybody. And that was that. Later, he and the twins became friends and hung around together sometimes.

"There was a group of us living in the neighborhood— Greg Arthur, Burt Round, Doug Rowley, Mike Petrillo. All those years, we'd play ball and do everything together, in and out of school. At Halloween, we'd take a match to a paper bag filled with dog crap that we'd put on peoples' porches, ring the bell and run. We'd toilet paper the trees at someone's house, and stuff like that—just mischievous and not destructive. Doug Rowley was a big guy, shy, with some kind of problem with his walking, and a few nervous habits like chewing on the inside of his cheek. The four of us had all talked about going into the military together, but as it turned out, we all went in at different times. Those were good friends. Those were happy days.

"I started out high school at Bishop Kelly, one of the few Catholic high schools in town. It was a good school really, and I learned a lot in the two years I was there. I don't know what it's like now, but about 1960, when I started, we were taught mostly by the Christian Brothers who came from Chicago. I liked most of them, with one memorable exception—Brother Henry. Doug Rowley happened to sit in front of me in his class. Brother Henry was a short stocky guy with an attitude. Well, one day, here's Doug Rowley chewing on the inside of his cheek as usual, and Brother Henry tells him to 'spit out the gum.' Doug told him he wasn't chewing gum. So Brother Henry tells him again and then begins to whack Doug across the hands with a rigid wooden pointer. Big as he was, Doug starts to cry because he doesn't know what to do. Well, I jumped my dumb ass up, grabbed Brother Henry by the collars and slammed him up against the blackboard, called him a little chicken shit, and told him if he ever touched Doug again, I was gonna whip his ass. So Doug and I both get sent to the Prefect of Discipline and then home. You know that time, both our dads went to the principal to back us up. Mr. Rowley sued and got some money for the abuse of his crippled son. Dad backed me up all the way on that one, oddly enough. I remember him telling me 'you should have gone ahead and kicked that brother's ass for picking on that boy.' Maybe Dad and I shared a few genes.

"There was my sister Karli who was two years ahead of me, then the twins Mike and Greg, about two years younger than me, then the little ones came along three and four years after that. It was always a circus around our house. Mom was sweet and cool-headed, and kept it all running.

"On the other hand, the old man was always riding the twins about something—it could be grades, getting a part time job, or getting chores done around the house. Worst of all, the old man been smoking forever, but swore that us kids wouldn't start. He'd get close to the twins, smell their hair or their breath, and off he'd fly on a rampage—the classic 'do as I say, not as I do' thing. How mindless was that? The twins were way too old to be getting whippings at thirteen or fourteen but out would fly his thin belt with a snap from his waist loops.

"'Bend over and grab those goddamn ankles!' He'd yell like a friggin' gunnery sergeant. Then, the same, 'How many times have I told you,' bullshit. Whack! Whack! Whack! It got to where the tears went fake as the twins could barely keep from laughing at each other during these punishments. Then the old man would try to figure out if they were already grounded for something else, or what might have an effect beyond the whipping. I'd already decided I was gonna take it to the old man someday for being so damned strict on the twins.

"Anyway, I'd had it one afternoon, and the old man and I got into a fist fight. Well, sort of. I charged him first and shoved him up against the trash cans in the back yard. Three or four of the lids went flying with a god-awful racket. He bounced back from the cans that were knocked over. The metallic clatter must have been heard up and down Marshall Street despite the closed windows, ceiling fans, and water coolers on that summer day. Then I started swinging. I kept hitting him—just not where I wanted to—landing all along his arms and shoulders, not his gut or head.

"You better settle down, now, Allison James," he said, "you're all riled up, and somebody's gonna get hurt!" I thought I'd won; that I'd whipped the old man's ass, and that's the way I'd planned to tell it. It occurred to me one night in my bunk in boot camp, that I had never landed a punch. While I had been wailing away, the old man had been kind and never threw a punch. He had been a boxer in his day at Tulsa Central High School, a kids program called Golden Gloves, and knew how to handle himself for a scrawny guy. I never really landed a good one.

"Don't know why I was hard-headed. I think I always felt defensive; I just felt I needed to grow up faster than I was. After the fight with the old man, I was so frustrated. My older sister Karli was in the Marines by then, so at seventeen, I asked the old man to take me down to enlist in the Marines, too. He didn't know what to do with me anymore and agreed."

Ψ

Skillfully, Miko had already developed his body language communication, transitioning from taking notes slumped in the ancient rotary desk chair to sitting erect. Placing the notepad to his right side signaled the end of active listening and on to planning what comes next.

"AJ, you know, you're like the perfect patient!" Miko commented glibly. "Our time is up at just the moment I'm going to ask you to tell me about your military years. That room that seems to have had deep consequences for the rest of your life. I'd like to go over that during our next visit."

"Ready when you are, Doc," AJ reported snappily. "Glad you think I'm perfect, you know, like most other people do."

CHAPTER 7
THE RECRUIT

AJ was consistently on time for his biweekly visits with Miko, a commitment that was noticed by the clinician. Each respected the other's time, regardless of what came out during the sessions as the relationship developed its own language and rhythm.

"Let's catch-up, AJ. How have you been since our last visit?" Miko asked, looking quickly over his prior notes.

"Not bad." AJ sidestepped the question. "I've been wondering where we're going with all these visits. What's the objective? Don't get me wrong, Doc, I've been enjoying our talks, and have probably learned a thing or two. But I feel like I've been skipping quite a bit of work by continuing to come here. The end goal is a bit foggy for me."

Miko smiled and drew himself closer to the desk. "AJ, you always seem to ask good questions. With emotional and mental health issues, it is foggy, to be frank, unlike sewing up a wound or setting a broken leg. As with any medical issue, we need to understand how the disorder started to get on the right path. Nothing we do here is magic. We have broad objectives—to feel better in those spheres of our lives where we are troubled, and through that, live better and happier lives. In the process, we pick up on a series of narrower objectives and just sort of hammer it out. We humans are full of surprises." Miko paused, then redirected. "When we started, if I may bring you back to that, you were brought in by the police; you didn't come on your own. You were armed. Those are concrete facts. We're now trying to understand who AJ Connelly is, and how he arrived in that situation. We don't have any concrete answer. Any layman—it doesn't take a policeman or a doctor—would think that can't be ignored; that there is a threat that remains unanswered. What I hope will happen is that by reviewing your experiences openly, we'll come to a better understanding of the elements of your life that can lead you away from destructive behavior."

AJ smiled and shook his head. "Well, who can argue with that? What do you want to ask me today?"

"Do you mind continuing to talk about periods of life that may have been particularly stressful? It may not all be pleasant, but my job is to help you see alternative views to what happens. For now, let's review your service time, from the beginning. It may take us a few sessions, but let's see how we do. Okay? You know my lack of military experience. So the burden is on you to be open and honest, and to help me understand. Think of it as if you wanted a young son or daughter to understand not only the circumstances, but how you reacted to those experiences. I'm sure in your work, as it is in mine, you get to know more when you are teaching. So, today, tell me about your Navy training."

AJ nodded agreement, and paused, noting the ill-defined unfamiliarity in the setting. Neither his wife nor the children of his blood had genuinely crossed this threshold. Now this stranger had asked to enter that room. And so he began.

"Probably because we lived in a more-or-less working-class neighborhood, the recruiting depot was just one more shop in a strip mall that I could have walked to from home. There was a poster of a mean-ass Uncle Sam on the store window—maybe you've seen it, Doc; it's part of our folklore of military recruitment—this old guy in a suit of the colors of our flag pointing a finger at everyone who looked and saying, 'I want you.' That time, I guess it was me he was pointing at. All the combat services, Army, Navy, and Marines, had recruiters in that one small office.

"When we arrived, a naval chief petty officer, what you call a CPO, greeted us, and explained the Marine recruiter had left the center for lunch. The CPO said we could wait for the Marine if we wanted. But then, as soon as he finished acting like the receptionist, his tone changed, and he invited Dad and me over to his desk.

"'Son,' he said, with my father sitting next to me, 'You don't want to join the Marines. You need to join the Navy!'

"'Yeah? And why's that?' I asked him, like any smart-assed, defiant kid.

"'Because, if you join the Marines, they'll send you to Okinawa or somewhere like that, and you'll spend two or three years right there and you're gonna do nothing.' The CPO paused. In retrospect, I think his recruitment style was to persuade through shock effect.

"'What do you mean—nothing?'

"'I mean nothing! Except just training. And you won't see a thing.' The CPO's hook was set and now would come the jerk. 'Man, you join the Navy, you get on a ship, son, and you're gonna go places—like Europe, Asia, and everywhere else. The Navy's going to train you to do a lot more than carry a weapon and clean latrines.'

"I bought into it and signed up right then. Dad had no problem with it. That's just how it happened. As I look back, man, Jesus was with me that day. My buddy Greg Arthur joined the Marines, was sent to Okinawa, and all he did was stay there and train, at least until Vietnam. The ripple effect of that Marine recruiter being out to lunch made all the difference in my military experience, and ultimately in my life. Four weeks later, I was gone!

"No sooner had the bus delivering the new crop of recruits pulled away from the parking lot at the receiving gate of Naval Training Station Great Lakes, when the training E-6, a Petty Officer First Class, began. Other ranking enlisted sailors filtered through our ranks making corrections on standing properly at attention, straightening gig lines—gig is the line-up of your buttoned shirt, your belt buckle, and your pants zipper line. They lost no time ordering the formation, getting our bodies in military semblance, you know, straight lines and rows—the ranks, even with us still in civvies—civilian clothes. The training and discipline started immediately, even while we were processing-in. I think, unless you come from a military family, it's a bewildering experience. Some guys wanted to run home to their mommas already.

"'You stupid pukes. All of you are stupid pukes. You could be somewhere else, doing something fun. But you are too stupid to figure that out. Hot damn! It doesn't get any more stupid than that. But no, all you sorry sacks of shit are lucky enough to have landed on my station. And worry of worries, the goddamn Navy expects me to teach you to look and act like sailors in ninety days. Most of you little girls won't last that long. But the few of you who do will be ready for the goddamn United States Navy. At that time, you will still be ignorant pukes. But do not despair. The Navy will train you and make you into something worthwhile for the first time in your sorry-ass lives. I and the exquisitely talented gentlemen circulating among you shapeless, worthless horse piss will show you how to stand up straight in straight rows. In the next ninety god-forsaken days, we will get your lazy asses into shape and provide your introduction to the dress, conduct, and operational language worthy of the US Navy so that you may begin this honorable journey that you have chosen to take. You will now take your instruction from my Senior Chief, who will have you fall in so as to be fitted for uniforms. You will keep it tight as you wait your turns, dick-to-butt, with your mouths shut! Senior Chief, they are now yours. Get these pukes out of my sight!'

"Anybody who's done boot camp will tell you that those three months were the longest single day of their lives. By the end of it, you are changed, programmed, and part of something. Just when you think you can't take any more, and you hate all these bastards who are constantly yelling at you, it all stops and you look at yourself in the mirror, and like what you've become. And you actually thank those sons of bitches and find a fondness for them.

"The next stop in the fall of 1963 was Barber's Point, Hawaii—Master at Arms Battery. In those days, that naval air station worked on organizing carrier air groups and squadrons for deployment to combat operations further west. I must admit it took a while to get my head around what that all meant, but in the next few months it would all come into focus. Mainly, the roles of each seagoing vessel and aircraft in a battle plan were sorted out there. Some new sailors like me, who would have critical roles, were sent there to learn how it all fits together. I was then shipped to the San Diego Fleet Anti-Warfare Training Center to learn what my job would be. I left there as a so-called Operational Specialist, lovingly known, in short, as a radar man. That job would put me in the combat information center (CIC), the beating heart of the destroyer. How I was chosen for that duty, I'll never know.

"The USS *Waddell* (DDG24) was laid down, meaning the first parts of what would eventually be the ship were set out at the shipyard, just one year before it was launched from Bremerton, Washington. Our newly formed crew picked up the sleek lady at her commissioning in August 1964. It was love at first sight, and my courtship was consummated during her shakedown—where you run the new ship through all its paces and test everything for ability and flaws. In speed trials, we were shooting the guns, testing all-weather, all-sea conditions, anti-submarine missile system, full anti-air capabilities. She had nuclear powered air torpedoes and regular torpedoes in her arsenal. Believe me, she was geared for what may come. The crew came together like magic. It was easy to feel invincible. I was close to nineteen when we got our orders for Vietnam. We escorted the flagship carrier Ticonderoga to the Western Pacific.

Ψ

Miko glanced at the storyboard of AJ's electronic record, adding up that this was the fifth or sixth follow-up since AJ's discharge to outpatient status. An awareness came to mind of the subtleties in psychotherapy discussed in department training conferences on recognizing when the barriers of resistance between patient and clinician give way to genuine communication and trust. Only now did Miko sense the story of self AJ had wrapped up inside would unfurl into this safe environment. This time, Miko focused ostensibly on his wristwatch. Timed to the moment when his patient might expect the familiar turn-off, he would open the gates. "Go on, AJ, please; this is interesting. I want to hear more."

AJ paused briefly before his pace of speech picked up.

CHAPTER 8
OPEN SEA

"**A**t times I've wondered, looking back over the time since leaving the Navy and the Vietnam War, I should have talked about it to people in a different way, you know—about the enjoyable parts first—the parts that really had nothing to do with the fighting. If I had, people may have gotten a better sense of how it was. And maybe they would have wanted to hear more.

"When I think about the good stuff, you know, I miss those days. After we'd had a last night of shore leave, usually involving honky-tonking and waking up dehydrated as hell, it felt good to get back at it. I had no dread of my duties on the ship. Typically, we'd be scheduled to weigh anchor from a port by 1100 hours, giving me time to grab my recovery breakfast of bacon and scrambled eggs, black coffee, and two slices of buttered toast. After that, I'd be ready to go, and I made it a point to be one or two steps ahead of the orders about to fly at us and all that came with it. . . ."

"'Mister Connolly, have you verified the schedule of contacts and completed all advisories for departure?' the officer of the deck would bark, running down his departure checklist.

"'Yes, sir. We have the harbor master's "go" to be underway at liberty through 1150 hours.'

"'Have you and your colleagues on the deck fully flushed any memories of your shore leave from recent and long-term memory and blown the tubes clear so as not to have any sorry-ass, lingering thoughts of ribaldry interfere with our customary smooth departure?' the lieutenant spouted, not masking his own yearning to be out there again.

"'Mister, we got shit to do!'

"'Sir, it would be presumptuous for me to speak for these other sacks of shit in your CIC. Maybe you ought to drop their asses for a butt load of push-ups or something like that to get their fannies in gear.' And I'd laugh like hell before a roar of back-talk would drown me out.

"Our first captain out on the *Waddell* had been a fidgety, hotheaded type who stomped around a lot. But for most of my time on the ship, we had Capt. Grant Walker. My god, what a fit captain! He was always calm, had superior seamanship skills, never showed fear, kept everyone else calm, and spoke to everyone as though he valued each one and the job they were doing. You wonder where that comes from—and you know you want some of it. I remember one time docked in the Philippines at Christmas; someone snuck a little bottle of booze into the CIC during my duty shift. Well, we got caught spiking our coffee with it by Capt. Walker. He just looked around the room and said, 'Merry Christmas, boys,' and moved on. Once the crew took up a collection and flew his whole family to meet him as a surprise when we were docked for a weekend in Hawaii. I'm sure I'm not the only one who thinks about him when I've had to exercise authority under pressure.

"When we weren't in combat, imagine the enlisted guys crawling the *Waddell* like a bunch of ants, doing chores, so that the three hundred fifty-five souls who rode her could co-exist.

Everyone but the officers and chiefs cleaned—compartments, decks, bathrooms. Other than my rounds on watch, my regular working day called for updating charts, navigation, and graphing, with no time to waste.

"Being busy without much down time would put me into a rhythm. We always had a destination and none of us questioned it. We just acted. There were times when it seemed like my destiny—like if I could, I would do this forever.

"Despite the ordinary routines, there was never an ordinary day at sea. There was so much to see and take in. Patterns of direction to wave sets, dolphins and an occasional whale dancing around the ship—a lot of things you might think of as random became organized in our observation and gave us a sense as to where we were in relation to land bodies and currents. The cooling, salt breeze and changing skies throughout the day gave you energy! The night sky seemed to come so close and tight as you could almost touch it, like it was weighed down by the billions of stars. I don't think you could ever see that anywhere but in that wilderness. Sunrises and sunsets rolled on, like living in a painting of the sky, clouds, and ocean constantly being done over. I never got tired of it—never bored or wanting something else. The rock and roll of storms—the distant lightning shows and riding the kick-ass typhoons—brought all my senses into balance, or so it seemed. I was a kid then, I guess. It was the right time. I look back on that now and realize the euphoria I had. I took it for granted then. Open water pacified me like a baby in a rocker. How could it not, when you felt you were exactly where you should be, doing exactly what you should be doing, all the time. I can't speak for everyone, but I'm sure most of us felt like we were the luckiest guys in the world.

"Our longest times continuously at sea were thirty-five to forty days. We were always going somewhere. If we weren't rescuing people, we might be getting ammo, food, or fuel off another ship—never just floating around in the water. You had a reason for every day. When an excursion was done and we were pulling into port, just like being at open sea, there was always something to look forward to. All over the Pacific Rim and the islands—so many days, I woke up in a new world. That was the Navy. If I'd gotten stuck on a base somewhere for four years, I'd have gone nuts. I found exactly what I needed, and in the balance, I was happy.

"I could have told the story that way when I got home, but then again, by the time I got home, nobody was asking, so I kept the good times to myself, just like the bad times.

"If I make it sound like all sweetness and light, let me be clear; we were at war. We didn't sing kumbaya. But it's probably important to know about the good stuff first, or a civilian won't understand the big picture. I can tell you some of what we encountered in combat so you can understand why we had to work so well together and do our jobs."

"AJ, this is a good time to stop and set up for our next visit. You know, I'm fascinated by your descriptions—you tell them very well," Miko encouraged, his interest genuine. "And of course, I do want to move on to your combat experiences at our next visit. Let me also ask you to fill in a gap for me. I've had a number of combat vets tell me that their war experience now seems like a different universe from their home life—like a nightmare that spills over into their daily thinking if they let it. Psychiatry is exploring how modern telecommunications may be changing the disconnect from home during the time in combat, but cell phones and computers weren't around when you were in the Navy—mainly just snail mail. I want to know if that disconnect influences your relationship with this past. I know that sounds a little vague, but you may know what I mean."

"Absolutely. We can talk about that next time." AJ responded distractedly, donning his jacket hastily. "Right now, I need to take a leak! Where's the nearest head?"

CHAPTER 9
EMPTY VICTORY

"**O**ne day during our first tour under Capt. Walker as CO, *Waddell* was under way to station at sea for sequential refueling and resupply, south of Yokosuka, en route to Honolulu. After glancing sideways through the door of the CIC on his way to the bridge, the CO stuttered-stepped and broke his stride. I think he must have caught me in the corner of his eye at my position, and was reminded of something that otherwise would not have occurred to him.

"'Connolly, finish what you're doing, then join me on the bridge, please,' he half-shouted to be heard from outside, yet in a tone he might have used in asking any piddly operations specialist to order him coffee during routine drill maneuvers.

"Having finished the communications to the supply vessels, I looked up and back to the officer of the deck who nodded me out the door; having heard the CO beckon. Through consistent attention to detail, and crisp communication during critical functions in the CIC, I had earned a level of trust. Jumping to attention just to maintain decorum would have been out of place. In the CIC and on the bridge, it was all business. On the job, most senior personnel reacted to me as they would to an inanimate instrument for decision-making and execution, totally different from downtime. I had no quarrel with that. Good leadership used talent where they found it, and that set well with me. Truth is, I had found myself in the Navy and it had found what I could do. Every day at sea, challenge and responsibility had absorbed all that rage and energy that had drove me to the recruiter's office. Mounting the bridge and speaking with the CO had become routine, and I was neither cocky nor shy about it.

"'Yes, sir.' I said.

"Capt. Walker looked away from the binoculars just long enough to make eye contact with me and then returned to the horizon. 'AJ, I want you to write a letter to your dad.'

"My habit of shifting my jaw just enough to chew on the inside of my cheek, when puzzled, was delayed until the captain looked away. With the CO, whatever the outcome of a conversation would be, you could be sure of brevity. You didn't stand there and mull things over when asked a question.

"'Sir, with respect, sir, I don't particularly want to do that,' I said, trying to sound matter-of-fact, but not defiant. Generally, the CO seemed emotionless. This time, I felt a genuine compassion from the CO—both for me and my dad—something beyond the duty of leadership.

"'Note from him indicates you've been deployed more than six months without a word from you. He's worried. You want to leave him worried?' This time the eye contact lingered a moment. Still, we both knew that this was not a direct order. 'I'd like you to write your father, AJ. That'll be all.'

"'Good evening, sir.'

"'Like' rather than 'want' conveyed a blend of nuances, as you can imagine, including (a) 'you don't know what it's like to be a father, so give the sucker some slack', (b) 'you're man enough to make the decision' and (c) 'this is not part of my duty nor your duty, but it's part of life.' The exchange was not off limits for either of us. Even at that age, I saw how the CO's experience guided his actions in dealing at the margins of duty and command. The matter was forgotten until the *Waddell* pulled into the yards at Honolulu to get fixed up. Still, I took it to heart and called home when we got in port.

"You asked about disconnect—I even got a name change in the Navy. At home, people called me by my middle name, Jamie, except when my parents were pissed, then it was the full-on 'Allison James.' Somewhere in the Navy, I became AJ, and I liked it, and it stuck.

"'Hi, Mom, it's Jamie. How are you?' It was funny how she went into a tizzy with the surprise call. Plunking a bushel of coins into the metal payphone was a chore, but I'd decided to not to ask to reverse the charges—to show the folks I was my own man.

"'Oh, my lord, Jamie! Why, it's so nice to hear your voice! Are you okay?' she clambered. 'Your daddy's not home and he'll be so mad that he missed your call. Where in the world are you?'

"'Hawaii, Mom. We're here for some routine maintenance on the ship. The captain said he got a letter from Daddy asking if I was okay, so I thought I'd call. Really haven't picked up any stationary yet, so thought I'd call. I've got a bag of quarters, so we're good for a few minutes. How is everybody?' I gushed a bit, surprised at how rich it felt to hear Mom's voice.

"'We're all fine here. The twins and the little ones are busy in school. We hear from Karli in Marine base Paris Island every couple of weeks. No one else is here, right now. Well, how are you?'

"'You know, Mom, I'm doing well. I like the Navy. I miss all you guys, but I'm seeing a lot and my job on the ship is actually kind of fun. Been to Tokyo and Okinawa, Hong Kong, Vancouver, Canada, and I've seen a lot of ocean! How's

Daddy? CO said he was worried, since I hadn't written. So I thought I'd call and let you know I was okay.'

"'Well, your daddy is okay,' she answered, betraying that there was more she wanted me to hear. 'He'd kill me for telling you, but, yes, he has been worried about you.'

"'Well, alright; tell me,' I might have taken the bit of pleasure about the old bastard suffering, now that I'd finally gotten free of him. But hearing it from Mom killed that joy.

"'Well, a few weeks ago he woke up in the middle of the night, kind of crying, which woke me up. He said he felt ashamed, like he'd pushed you away, and pushed you into the service from the two of you not getting along. It's really eating at him. You know, with all the TV news about more and more boys getting killed or wounded in Vietnam, if something happened to you, well, he doesn't know how he'd ever forgive himself,' her voice and small sniffles got to me. 'Jamie, I don't think you realize how much your daddy loves you and what you mean to him. Lord, the both of you can be so hardheaded! It's time for that to stop!'

"'Really, Mom, he was crying? He said all that?' my grip on the phone tightened.

"'Yes. I'm so glad you finally called. He'll be tickled to know that you're okay. He's out buying some tools or something. I'm so aggravated that he missed your call. You know he collects everything he can find about your ship. He gets these little newsletters from the Navy about your ship, but it's not personal.'

"The call for more coins from the telephone gave me a moment to absorb. I plunked in all I had left buying two more minutes. 'Momma, I love you both with all my heart. I love all you guys. Daddy didn't push me in. We were both pushing at each other. Momma, would you tell Daddy for me that I love him, and I miss all you guys? Tell Daddy the Navy is treating me good and I'm doing well. And I will write him a letter soon.'

"'Jamie, I will tell him what you said. You know your father has a temper that wraps him up in knots, and then he pays for it later. It breaks my heart when there's quarreling among you all. But he loves me and all you kids more than you'll ever know. When you're feeling lonesome out on that ship, you remember that, alright? And you promise me you'll be careful and get yourself home here as soon as you can.'

"I wrote a letter that day, page after page, everything I could think to write about—how he was a good father to us kids—that I just needed to stand back far enough to see it. I went on about my training, and what I could say about what we were doing. A lot was classified, and I didn't want to compromise my clearance. The Navy reads some of the letters.

"That call kept me up a few nights in the rack in that brief shore leave. It hurt me to think of the old man being all eaten up, when I was loving the life I was leading. I wasn't gonna let that go on any longer. It got me thinking about things I knew but had never really thought about. How the old man's father walked out on him and his two little brothers and their momma when Dad was thirteen; how he had to work to help support them all and that kept him from going to college. He had mentioned all that but never dwelled on it. One of his biggest life disappointments had been getting ruled physically unfit for flat feet during WWII—he had tried to enlist three separate times. I'd heard all that before, but until that day, I just thought, well, that's the old man's problems. Once, Daddy had some business trip to Long Beach while we were in port there. I was on shore leave when he came to visit the ship. Someone else showed him the CIC and all around the ship. I would have been so proud to be the one to show him around. It was a chance of a lifetime that slipped by.

"I got home only once in the four years I was on active, between '63 and '67. We were so busy on the *Waddell*. But it was that call when I realized how much he loved me. And from then on, we got along fantastically! When he got older and retired to take care of Mom with her Alzheimer's disease, he took great care of her. He had re-engineered his old car to hold a wheelchair and had built an escape hatch through their bedroom wall at the front of the house so he could drag her helpless body out if they had a fire. Sometimes, I'd drive out there to watch Mom so he could get out, or Karli would watch Mom, and I'd take Dad to a movie or shopping.

"When he died, and I went through his things, he had all kinds of my stuff there—pictures I'd sent him, and some that the ship had sent him. He had all that stuff. But I never found that first letter. I wonder what he did with it."

CHAPTER 10
FLINT RIVER 605

"**W**hen we were in formation with a carrier, one of my jobs was to screen returning aircraft coming back to the carrier to make sure they were ours, otherwise I'd shoot them down. The North Vietnamese had Russian MIGs that would try to sneak in with our returning and get a shot at the ship formation. Our pilots were supposed to send a signal called a squawk when we asked for it. Once, I almost shot down a returning fighter bomber of ours who wouldn't squawk until the last second. I'd have never lived that down even though I would have been justified in protecting the fleet.

"After all these years, I remember the call name of our first fighter reconnaissance aircraft to go down—*Flint River* 605, an RA-5C. Sometimes, I can't remember what I had for breakfast, yet some things from the war are like they happened today. Events happen fast and get stacked together; you hardly have time to breathe. Afterward, you run them through your mind over and over, looking for something you could have done. The day gets burned into your brain.

"The recon flight radioed, 'Base, this is *Flint River* 605. Request clearance for additional pass. I think there's more intel we can bring back. Over.'

"'Uh, yeah, *Flint River*, this is base. If skies are clear, proceed with a final pass, then return to base. Over,' came the order.

"Newly assigned to the carrier Kitty Hawk, Lt. Gerald Coffey and his navigator Lt. Bob Hansen sensed these reconnaissance fly-overs were a lead-up to something major. Scuttlebutt had it that North Vietnamese shore batteries were becoming more active, and one thing would lead to another. On the carrier deck, the two naval aviators learned the day's recon objectives would be tomorrow's targets of the first US naval shore bombardment campaign in the conflict.

"The enemy cannons were ready for *Flint River*'s second reconnaissance pass and opened-up on those guys—big time.

"What sounded like a hammer striking a metal pipe over the radio sent the RA-5C into an uncontrolled barrel roll, devolving into a spiral as the fighter raced toward blue water, ultimately exploding as it hit the water east of Nghe An Province, near Cape Bouton. No parachutes were deployed.

"The *Waddell* CIC was tuned in on air-to-carrier communications and heard a message from a fleet escort aircraft. 'Base, we are picking up a radio beep in the area where *Flint River* 605 went in. Uh, bad as it looked, someone has got to be moving there. Closing approach for visual, over.'

"The CIC com phone rang in its expected interval. The chief had a habit of nodding every time he said, 'Yes, sir,' to the bridge when it meant a change in activity. The crew of the CIC was cocked and ready to respond to any anticipated search and rescue (SAR) call.

"'Ladies, you heard it,' the chief made clear. '*Brinkley Bass* and *Waddell* will head to the crash water at full speed. The same spotter IDed two sizable enemy junks headed there, one from the north and the other from the south, so we are in a race. I need your full attention: we can expect a lot of shit from those shore batteries. A Huey MEDEVAC chopper has just taken off the carrier Ranger, so that crew be there first; we'll back them up. Look sharp!'

"These were the times when it got real. The rest of the world disappeared. Seconds ticked by in slow motion; nothing got by me. Sweat was the cool friend it was meant to be.

"North Vietnamese mobile cannon shore batteries would be firing on all friendly forces running up and down the coast. Their targeting equipment wasn't great, but if they had any sweet spot for targeting at all, it was right at the range where the *Flint River* crew went down. *Waddell* and the other destroyer, *Brinkley Bass*, were dodging the full wrath of those mobile batteries as we approached. The *Waddell* bridge officers closed their binoculars on the hovering Huey. Just as the cable was being lowered to the personnel in the water, the Huey took a direct hit mid-fuselage, putting the technician out of action and rendering the Huey uncontrollable and limping to its own demise five miles east. A second SAR helicopter had diverted from the crash site of *Flint River* aircraft to pick up the surviving pilot and co-pilot of the first Huey.

"Amid the heavy shelling and return fire between destroyers and shore, the *Brinkley Bass* connected on the junk approaching from the north and lit it up like a torch and sank it. As the scene cleared, the *Waddell*'s bridge could see the junk inbound from the south was drawing out a single naval aviator, making the live capture. It was all the two destroyers could do to return defensive fire to shore, and to align their evasive zig-zagging when orders came from Task Force Command to break off.

"Coffey was in the hands of the North Vietnamese; Hanson had not survived the crash. Of all the skirmishes I remember, that was the most intensive fire *Waddell* came under. There were so many shore batteries firing on us, the seas around us spewed like a swimming pool in a hailstorm from the shore artillery from just about every caliber you can name. So many subsurface explosions one after another—boom, boom, boom, boom, boom—was deafening! We had to pull back. How we came away unscathed was a miracle. Even though I kept my focus, I could still feel myself shaking nearly a half hour after we were out of range. It was also the singular rescue we didn't complete. Command will always decide not to risk a destroyer carrying three-hundred fifty-five lives to pick up one. No one could rescue Coffey, and that sucked. A couple of other aviator crewmen died that day from the first Huey that was downed. Those losses can pile up on you, especially when you're so close to the save. The good part is that Coffey survived and was eventually repatriated to the US. He lived to write and speak about his experiences."

"You've gone into a lot of detail, AJ, on this particular rescue effort, when the *Flint River* crew was shot down. Why do you remember so much about it?" Miko grimaced, probing to fill his own gap of understanding. "It sounds like it did not go as well as most search and rescue attempts you were involved with. Why is this the one you wanted to talk about?"

"Yeah, I know, to most military folk, the successes seem less important than the failures, right? I've heard all that." AJ stood up, slipped his hands in his pockets, turned to the windows and stared down silently at the parking lot below. "I think it was the helplessness. We ran to save our butts. Yeah, it was the right decision. Still, I think maybe everyone is haunted by someone left behind or something left undone. It's an empty spot that never gets filled in, no matter what the mind tells you. There's no good place to put the anger and regret, when it comes to mind. I guess everyone who wasn't there gets to be a target for the anger and resentment. Ha," AJ joked. "Now I'm the shrink, telling you!"

Miko smiled softly and nodded the affirmative.

"I don't know." AJ slid a palm down the side of his face, across the mouth and down the front of his neck and gently chewed on his inner right cheek. He paused, rubbing hands together, noting a perceptible tremor. "I don't let it get to me." AJ rubbed the knuckles of a tight fist in the opposing palm. "Hey, are we done for today?"

"Is it that you collectively ran from a fight, and that's just not you? I mean, AJ, you heard over the radio the shots that brought the *Flint River* down," Miko slipped in.

AJ fiddled with the zipper of the insulated Dickies work jacket that was his trademark apparel on all but the most frigid fall and winter mornings. "Yeah, I think we're done for today."

CHAPTER 11

JALAPEÑOS AND COFFEE

Natalia welcomed the rush of warm air through Walmart's automatic doors against the early October chill. Only last week she had complained about summer's sticky humidity. She greeted several strangers between the entrance and commandeering a grocery cart from the stacks.

When these moments presented themselves, Natalia would embrace them, and wall herself off in the anonymity. Isolated in foot traffic, she was now mercifully alone. She had just left her perpetually complaining mother at the care home, too worn out after the trip to her internist to go shopping today. No grandchild in tow, no husband to scoff at her choices, no one to answer to—intercalated and precious were these healing moments of solitude. She did not waste them when they appeared, and would relish existence in the temporary bubble, even if there were only a few things she needed to pick up today. People hustling by in the aisles may or may not smile, or notice hers given freely, carrying on their lives on other wavelengths, separate. Natalia imagined that each kept their pain to themselves, as if it did not exist nor matter.

"Excuse me."

Natalia turned to the soft voice that gently interrupted the spell. The slim woman's olive complexion, absent any Native American features, seemed out of place in Oklahoma. "Can you tell me about these vegetables?" she asked, holding differing varieties of jalapeños in two hands—green, red, and ghost peppers. "I hear they are popular in this country, but I don't know them to cook, yet."

"Oh, my dear, then it's good that you asked! Most people just call these hot peppers. They get chopped up and added to a lot of dishes to make them spicy. Better be safe and take the red ones to try first. The green ones are more intense. These little ghost peppers will set you on fire!" Natalia giggled, her whole face smiling.

The girl's own smile rose only gradually under pensive eyes and a wrinkled forehead, signaling that not all had been understood. Natalia studied the girl's face and tried to place the accent; it was not quite the Italian of Natalia's mother, yet still mildly familiar. "Where do you come from, sweetie?"

"Oh, thank you. My English is not perfect, even after a long time of study. Yes, I am from Greece, from the south part. I join my husband when his new job start. He works at the big Public Health Hospital and his English is almost natural now." Bia halted her gush, not to impose on the surprisingly kind stranger. "So I try the red ones first, yes?"

"Well, aren't you precious! You're a long way from home. And that's so funny—I was just recently at Public Health when I took my husband in for a visit with his doctor there. Maybe you know him, Dr. Papa—jeez, something like Papa Joe, I'm not sure."

Bia's eyes grew wide. "No, no, maybe Papagiannis you meet? Miko Papagiannis?" she asked as she carefully sniffed the peppers. "This is my husband! He trains there now in psychiatry."

"Well, I'll be! I think that's it. And he's a psychiatrist? I can't believe it. Is this a coincidence or what? My husband has been seeing him since early summer and says that the doctor might want to talk to me at some point." Natalia lowered her voice for privacy as well as dramatic effect and wagged her head side-to-side. "You know, my husband would never see a shrink—not until he had to. But I think AJ—that's what people call my husband—AJ really likes him. And I hope it's going to be good for him. AJ is a very hard-headed man."

"Of course, Miko cannot talk to me about his patients, so I don't know anything. Yes, this is a big city, so what is the probability that we meet? And thank you about the . . . the . . . how you say . . . jalapeños."

Natalia sensed Bia's awkwardness, a reserved politeness and a loneliness. An image of her mother, once a war bride, crossed her mind. This odd encounter could be a pleasant distraction, if she were careful not to make it all about AJ. "You know, I have a little time and just a few things to get. Would you like to have a cup of coffee? There's a Starbucks in the other corner of this store. If you have time, let me buy you coffee. Gee, it feels like a vacation meeting a person from Greece!"

Bia slowly smiled and nodded. "You are so kind! I have little talk with Americans about the simple things! "Yes, perhaps I see you back there in, erm, ten minutes, after I get a few things. My name is Bia. And yours?"

"Bia, that's so pretty!" Natalia affirmed, smiling widely. "I'm Natalia. Okay then, I'll see you soon!"

Ψ

Bia drew a nasal breath and pursed her lips as she sat down with Natalia, bracing for the first moment she would struggle for an English word, knowing that encounters like this were what she needed most to hone her ability with the language.

The acquaintances she had made at work in the past year seemed aloof, more like Europeans, who were fine with the exclusion of other nationalities in their social circles. She tried not to stare at Natalia who was sporting tidy white slender jeans and a billowy cotton blouse gathered at her narrow waist. She seemed to lack any pretense, as if she could talk to anyone like an old friend.

"Well, tell me a little bit about how you guys wound up here in Tulsa? Why not one of the big cities like New York or Chicago?" Natalia asked. "And what are you doing when your husband is at work? Do you have kids?"

Cringingly, Bia migrated first to the universal identifier for women—maternal status—although she was past resenting the pancultural practice. "No kids, not yet," she replied. "We came here because the residency position was open in the public hospital. It is not a famous place so much, but the training in psychiatry is supposed to be very good. Miko feels very, how you say, lucky, to get this post."

"Well, I know we aren't supposed to talk about patients, but my husband AJ seems to be having some depression. He has a drinking problem that maybe got started when he was in the Navy during the Vietnam War. He has so much anger in him. I'll never understand. I hope he's not going to be a burden for your husband. And, anyway, we don't need to talk about my husband!" Natalia inhaled the steam rising from her coffee.

Bia, sensing her own isolation in the self-effacing older woman, smiled graciously. "It's what Miko is training to do. He says problems of the mind and spirit are as painful as other illnesses and can lead to death if not helped. So I hope your husband can get better."

"That's so interesting," Natalia endorsed. "My husband is like so many others who came back from Vietnam. So many were angry and violent. My father met my mother in Italy when he fought in World War II there. He never talked about the war but treated my mom like a princess. Back then, men came home from World War II as heroes and got good jobs and got on with life. Vietnam was something different, I guess. It's confusing. I really don't want to hear about it. My dad was just a simple man and never drank much. I don't understand why more Vietnam vets can't just be like him." Natalia paused before drawing a sip of coffee. "There I go again! Sorry to go on about something that probably means nothing in Greece! How did your husband decide to be a doctor?"

"Oh, it is kind of long story," Bia's eyes searched over Natalia's head, not anchoring on any of the signage for the sales on produce and canned goods. "Miko has a kindness. He was not considering medicine when he was in *lykeio*, kind of like your high school, where we met. He was wanting to be a writer when he was a boy, but he did so well in all the compulsory math and sciences, everyone pushed him to study medicine. So did I, when we got to know each other. I think the writing is not very secure, but in medicine, especially in America and Europe, the money becomes regular. Maybe Miko agreed on science to make me happy. He does very well, so far, in his training. It seems natural to him, but sometimes he still misses the writing."

"Well, I think either would be a fascinating life work, not like a housewife or a preschool teacher like me!" Natalia giggled. "Are you working here?"

"Actually, it took a long time to receive a work visa and the green card, but now I'm working at the OSU medical center in recruitment and admissions for the Master's programs. I have a degree in accounting, but do not have accounting certification here. This job uses some of my education, like a bookkeeper, not the tax and investment parts, so there will not be much advancement for a long time. Anyway, you see, I must be the practical one in my little family!" Bia summed up without bitterness.

"Wow," Natalia marveled. "You two must be so smart! Well, good for you!" She glanced at her Timex and then at her waiting grocery cart. "Well, Bia, I'd better be going. It's been so nice to meet you! I shop here a lot, and maybe we'll run into each other again. I'm not going to tell AJ that I met you—not yet—he'll think I've been snooping somehow."

"Very nice, Natalia! Ciao!" Bia rose, processing the part about 'snooping.' "Hope to see you again, as well."

CHAPTER 12

COLLISION COURSE

Miko had made it through his first Midwestern winter last year sticking with the full-length wool frock that suited most Mediterranean winters just fine. Having judged the increasingly popular puffy coat to be of dubious couture, he was beginning to have second thoughts as the Oklahoma black ice was laying in ahead of the holiday season. No one here, he imagined, would appreciate his languishing about clement December days in Vathi when Norwegians would pepper the village on extended weekends, their daylight and temperatures growing ever more minimal. AJ showed up in the same Dickies jacket he had worn at his previous visit. Miko chose not to comment on his own seasonal suffering to the combat veteran.

"For a while now, we've gone into the room of your military years. As your own experience has borne out, AJ, one of the aspects that makes this time of life so consequential is that it most often marks the beginning of independence from family. It can be a very intense time of life with so many adjustments happening." Miko paused after framing. "Last visit, when we talked about the *Flint River* rescue, it was the first time I recall a visceral reaction from you toward a memory. I hope it wasn't too upsetting to you. This is the type of insight we're on a mission to expose."

"Hmm," AJ mumbled, without a notion of assent. "Yeah, well, I've began to wonder again where we're going; what's the end game? We've been at this nearly six months. Don't get me wrong, you've been a good listener, better than other civilians, and you've taken an interest. Seems like you do your homework and know what you're doing. So far, it's going alright, and you haven't seriously pissed me off—yet!" AJ grinned. "And that's good! But, overall, I'm not sure I'm feeling any different. Maybe I'm expecting too much."

"I get it, AJ. Certainly, it wouldn't do either of us any good if I piss you off," Miko frowned and grinned back. "But try to remember, my job is not like your job as an electrician where you can see where you want to go and how to get there. My job has some framework, certainly, but it's always an exploration, because, you know, patients don't read the textbook, and they all insist on being different. What's with that?" Miko was relieved when AJ chuckled at his attempt at humor in English. "So it's hard to be explicit about where our interactions may take us. We just keep our eyes and our minds open, and work at it."

Miko got no push-back. This point of frustration had arisen in many patients during his rookie months and he was feeling better at navigating it. He continued. "Today, I want to go back to that room and open some more closets and drawers. Pointedly, when I bring up the word 'fear,' what is the first memory to surface for you around that word?"

"In the Navy?"

"Yes, in the Navy—unless another incident you associate with feeling fearful is more prominent."

AJ's gaze wandered gradually upward, eventually fixing on the large clock. He reached around to scratch his right flank momentarily before crossing his arms. His breathing deepened as he straightened in the chair and began to speak.

"You know, when the ship's alarms go off anywhere near you, it pierces like a dagger through both ears into the brain, like sending a shock of electricity to the tips of your fingers and feet. Those alerts have to exceed the noise of wind, waves, engine, and maybe even artillery fire. If it isn't heard, lives may be lost. I was half-asleep in my rack, and, good god, when the alarm went off before we hit, I jolted up and hit my head so hard on god-knows-what, I saw stars. Everywhere I looked eyes and mouths were wide open. I was kind of disoriented, not knowing if I'd just laid down from my shift or if I had been in my rack for hours. All of a sudden came the unmistakable deep-throated clunks of the automated locking mechanisms on all exits of the compartment. Training algorithms flashed through my mind, but no one needed to tell me that this wasn't a drill. Only a few hours before, we had just emerged undamaged from the pounding of shore battery salvos during that failed attempt to recover the *Flint River* crew. *Waddell* was sidled up to the *Navasota*, along with the *Brinkley Bass*, for refueling at the end of my last watch in the CIC. Nothing should be more ho-hum than that.

"'All hands, stand by, and brace for collision,' came the announcement. You could hear a bit of panic in the conn's voice, meaning whoever is in control of the ship's movements at any moment. By then, most seaman were on their feet. You'd be amazed how quick sailors can fly out of a narrow rack from a dead sleep. There they stood, silent, listening.

"I guess a few seconds had ticked by, and some of us began to breathe again in the hope that the hit may have been avoided. The impact then shook us like ragdolls. Everything loose in the compartment—radios, tape decks, pens, paper, laundry, you name it—became projectiles smashing everywhere. Guys were bounced off anything immobile, the jar jerking their grips loose from bars and whacking heads, shoulders, knees into racks or whatever, and a half-dozen guys to the floor. Then came this god-awful metallic grind—like a scream from some beast in pain, deafening, almost paralyzing—then fading to a high-pitched whine, along with a series of whumps, shuddering everything, one after another. Then everything went dead except for the regular on-and-off whoop of the alarm. The compartment lights went dim, then red, leaving all of us frozen in this sort of unreal portrait. I tell you, nearly thirty men, left to their imaginings, went silent and focused on any information that might come over the call. Then the chatter broke out.

"'God damn, what just hit?' 'What the fuck?' 'Son-of-a-bitch!' like a bunch of cackling jungle birds.

"With my experience in the CIC, I was used to being the one who found the answers, not waiting for others to get information to me. But I had no trouble getting guys attention when I needed to. What didn't need to be said in that moment was what everybody knew—that the ship had a superb safety crew who, as a routine response to damage, would seal off any number of compartments to keep the vessel afloat. They do that to save ship and maximum lives; there have been incidents when some crew in non-critical chambers might be sacrificed. Well, I thought the best control of the situation would be to talk to them like sailors, like talking frankly would keep everyone calm. I think I was nineteen or twenty at the time.

"'Listen up, shit-heads!' I shouted, and acted like I was somehow in charge, 'Any of you pukes see any water incursion anywhere? Look around, dummies—up and down. Are we watertight?'

"'All is dry over here, sir!' came the first response. Someone was so shook-up, he was calling me, a lowly E-3, 'sir'. You could hear scuffling shoes and knees and eyes inspecting from floor to top. 'None, here.' 'We're dry!' The next thirty seconds accounted for our status.

"'Okay,' I said. 'Stand by and keep your shit together. We're secure. When I came in, we were refueling—not under any fire, and well out of range.'

"Thank god, we got a clear voice from the conn just after that —'Damage assessment underway. All hands stand by. Compartments report any casualties ASAP.'

"Some guys rolled back into bunks, while most just stood, not yet ready to relax. My head was going at a hundred miles an hour, figuring all the possibilities, and what each one meant to us in lockdown there. I could see myself doing this mental exercise as I did it; it was an odd feeling.

"I remember thinking, if this is where it ends, then this is a real piece of shit. That thought was at one end of the possibilities for our outcome. We all eventually read about the destroyer USS *Evans* that was cut in two by the Aussie carrier Melbourne, the bow section taking a hundred or more sailors to their deaths in a heartbeat that day. Could just as well have been us. You know, we'd been, as they say, 'shot at and shit at,' by the enemy, damn near every working day we were out there, and came away from it without a goddamn scratch.

"Even when you tell yourself to focus, when the shit gets real, your mind races in all directions. My last letter to Dad would probably get there this week. Next, I'm thinking, is anyone especially pissed off at me right now that I should have squared with? I guess it may be important to me to die with a clean slate. If I die here in this compartment, then it is what it is. No fault of my own—died in the course of duty. I can live with that—or die with it, in this case. I had hoped for more. It sure would be nice to see Natalia again, and hug everybody. But I signed up for this—no good to piss and moan. If we run out of air, I'll just go to sleep. Drowning is the worst! Looks like that's not going to happen right now, thank god. Shit, where am I at with god? Haven't given Him much thought in a long time, but I've done plenty of drinking and fist-fighting and chasing tail. Please forgive me for all the dumb-shit stuff I've done, and whoever I've hurt. Please don't let me suffer long, if it comes to that. Those were my thoughts. I'll bet most of the guys in the compartment were either thinking the same kind of stuff, or maybe they had sucked up my calming bull-shit, and were thinking they were just going to get another hour of rack time before this passed.

"Looking around, some were chatting in twos and threes. Some put pen to paper. A few had balled-up in their racks. A few had stretched out in them, mostly staring straight up, hands behind their heads, like in a trance. It didn't take long after the hatches were locked and ventilation was suspended for the sweat to start dripping, breathing more labored, and pulses to rise. I found myself moving slowly between the rows of berths, checking on the guys with cuts on a scalp or a nose, guarding a knee or an elbow. My thinking we might all die there set me to looking for any young guys that needed comfort—someone else's little brother, maybe—what I hoped someone might do for my little brothers Mike and Greg on their ship in these circumstances, even though they were pretty tough on their own. Maybe there was some redemption to be found in these moments, if it would help. This was not a time for criticism of anyone. I was still young myself, going on twenty, and for some of these other kids, that was senior enough—if you could act that way.

"Anyway, the worst didn't happen. The damage assessment went fast, and we were out in about an hour and a half. What had happened was a junior officer at the conn of *Brinkley Bass* had lurched forward on the exiting formation after emerging from the routine resupply formation with the *Navasota* there in the Gulf of Tonkin. The CO relieving that lieutenant JG after the collision warning had gotten confused and ordered a hard right turn. The *Brinkley Bass* stern ground right into the *Waddell* at midship, and ripped a jagged line through the hull, spewing a huge rooster tail of steel sparks fanning a hundred feet into the night sky. That was how it was described by a sailor on deck during the event. The *Navasota's* repair crew battled through the night and kept the listing *Brinkley Bass* afloat. Instead of total disaster for both destroyers, no sailor was lost, happily, including my sorry ass. Anyway, that's how the write-up came out. Barely a footnote in a wartime log from 1966, that was the one time I truly thought I may be seeing my last hours. You'd think that experience would have made me a better man forever, and not just until the next shore leave."

"Do you think about this often now, AJ? Have you shared this with your family?" Miko asked.

"No, that memory has not really come up during the day, but it has been one of those recurring nightmares." AJ's speech slowed to his usual pace. "I usually just wake up in a panic because my heart's beating faster or I get a little bit nauseated, almost always around a quarter to three in the morning, oddly enough. In the dream, I still think this is the end, over and over. It's not pleasant; I never get to resolve anything. Natalia and the kids don't like the scary stories, so telling them doesn't go anywhere. Every combat vet I know has their own stories— they know the feelings you have without you saying anything. They know terror. It's their knowing that means something, and that's why there's that comradery. For a lot of guys, even that's not enough for them to keep it together. If you're a vet from Vietnam, everybody else would just prefer you keep quiet. We are part of a nation's shame. Think about that. But then, you're not an American, are you, Doc?"

"That's right, AJ, and maybe that allows me to think neutrally, and be interested only in you, not the outcome of the war." Miko replied. "Has the comradery of combat veterans been good for you?"

"Absolutely, but then again, here I am with you! So there must be things I still need to work on, to be where I want to be." AJ knew Miko's routine of closing-up—putting the desk in order, setting the next visit, as he was doing now. "You know, people everywhere look to America as a good country, an example of what could be, and hope for it to succeed. And some curse America because it exists, and they can't get to it. But I won't go off on philosophy since we're done for today."

"Thank you for that, AJ," Miko smiled. "This is not about understanding other countries and vice-versa, AJ. That's not my expertise. Right now, it is about understanding you. Next time, I want us to explore your experience with losing someone you knew personally. Give that some thought, will you? Let's arrange our next meeting for after the holidays."

CHAPTER 13
SEA DRAGON

The chill of gray, leafless winter had resumed its austere authority over life in Tulsa. The passage of last year's memories and family holidays met mid-January's indifference. This imposing season of realism put Miko into a strange contemplative mood. He welcomed it. Waking-hour dreads had lost their bitterness. Springtime was too distant to rouse hope. Miko strode to work, pondering the logic and the nature around him. How would he write about this feeling, if he were writing? Now was the essence of what we are, stripped bare of want, where the deepest core of the spirit is found calm, undisturbed by longings for cyclic reprieves. He faced a new day with a long list of patients to be tended. He felt fortunate, and hoped this elation would not crumble under the burden of caring.

AJ would be his first clinic patient today. Miko's professional boundaries had formed adequately. By now, nonetheless, patient names on schedules could evoke a visceral response, even before his mind could recall a diagnosis or a face. Miko looked forward to seeing AJ Connelly, though in no academic sphere would this non-descript patient ever be fodder for a teaching presentation. The competitive intellectualization of the rare cases, those mostly a matter of pharmacologic ingenuity and compliance, no longer enticed Miko. The untouchable ethos of the individual person who blended into the crowd, whose pain may erupt unexpectedly, had begun to captivate his attention. Well into the middle year of the training requirement and steeped in practical psychiatry, he was grasping the art of relative neutrality, of creating a safe therapeutic atmosphere that neither provoked decompensation nor stifled the free-flow of thought from his patients.

"Good morning, AJ." Miko greeted unassumingly. "Do you remember what I asked you to think about for this discussion?"

"Sure do, Doc." The older man drew four-folded pages from a hip pocket and began straightening them. "As a matter of fact, I've copied something I wrote for the *Waddell* blog online several years ago. It's kind of odd; all these guys have been off the *Waddell* for decades, but folks can still read about it online and share stories of their times and shipmates. It's kind of an unspoken agreement that it has to be written in pretty good grammar, so I printed this out and jotted some things in the margin. If you don't mind me reading some of it, I'll tell you about losing someone I knew in combat. Are you okay with that?"

"Certainly, AJ. You know our time limits. You can read or just talk as you like. I'll ask questions where I need to. I don't want us to be confined to something written a long time ago, but, yes, writing can certainly help us organize what we need to say. Go ahead." Miko put down his pen and assumed a comfortable slouch in the desk chair.

"Well, a signalman first class named Grable sidled up to me at the taffrail. Both of us were on break after course and heading were set in leaving Naval Station Long Beach that morning. I took the smoke he offered me and thanked him.

Neither of us felt the need to converse much. At that time, even if we knew next to nothing about some guy on the ship, we were like brothers.

"The *Waddell* had recently concluded seven months in the Long Beach yard for structural repairs following the collision with the *Brinkley Bass*, beyond the Band-Aid patch-up in Subic Bay. Regular hours and a lot of shore leave had been good, yet there was excitement among the crew to finally be underway. Fleet and independent training exercises along the Southern California horizon had limbered the old girl up, so to speak, and the *Waddell* leaned into what awaited us. You remember days like that. The late March afternoon sun had burned off an overcast morning, the sky broken up here and there with stratus clouds—nothing but silver-blue seas gleaming on our path to the horizon. It felt good to be headed back.

"Grable started to say something when the alert whistle sounded.

"'Now hear this, now hear this: Stand by for instructions from the CO.' Too close-up, the squawk was deafening, not much less than the general alarm.

"The CO laid out where we were headed. 'Gentlemen, after refueling at Midway, Operations Tactical Command has us joining naval gunfire support for the marines and their ARVN counterparts south of the DMZ in the mouth of the Cua Viet River, under the call name Operation Beacon Hill. We will be supplying suppression fire, along with a battery of destroyers and cruisers, using principally five-inch fifty-four-centimeter rounds. Our objective is to provide rest for our troops through harassment fire, and to retard the enemy, primarily NVA sappers attempting to infiltrate the lines, blow-up munitions, and do damage to our people. Within our range, we intend to keep the unseen enemy guessing by scattering rounds within their domain of operations and occupation. Our marines are engaging the enemy daily. They depend on our activity to sustain the effort. Good luck, gentlemen, and happy hunting. CO out.'

"The journey was interrupted by running aground at Midway, but the lay-up of four weeks at Pearl Harbor for hull repairs didn't dent our enthusiasm. The agility of the *Waddell* and the crew soon paid off in the inland waters of the Cua Viet River. The NVA were stymied by constant interference from the *Waddell*'s random shelling. In the CIC, I had a continuous front row seat to the ongoing action. Back at the four-hour shifts on duty, four hours in the rack and some chow, I felt normal again, back to the way we lived while underway.

"'Dear Mom and Dad,' began my at-least-once-a-month letter. Laying in my rack, I could usually bang out something in the fifteen minutes it would take to doze off. What do you say when you can't tell your folks that you're shooting guys on the beach who are trying to sneak around the marines . . . 'Hope you are fine. I'm doing well. After leaving Long Beach, we stopped for supplies and fuel at Midway and spent some time in dry dock at Pearl. Got the pictures from your trip to Arizona. Let me know what you hear from the twins." My dad understood the code—the small talk was meant to say, 'I'm alive and able to write at this moment.' That, and 'I love you and miss you,' was enough.

"Suppression fire . . . Rack time usually went better if I posted the idea in my head of what I could expect to wake up to. Suppression fire led to thoughts of marines. For me, the Marine Corps was personified by Greg Arthur, my elementary school pal who had enlisted in the Marines shortly after I had gone to sea. Greg Arthur—the name that always came out as one word to distinguish the schoolmate from my brother Greg. Greg Arthur had always been a bit more schoolish than me. Damn near everyone liked him. Greg Arthur played a good game of baseball, never bragged, and would stick up for anyone being picked on. We hadn't had contact in years,

Greg Arthur made it all real—what we were doing to create cover for the marines on shore. If nothing else, that's what I was there to do—to have Greg Arthur's back, and anyone like him. Sailors in the CIC weren't saturated with the fear that arose from being in the middle of the daily carnage. But the soldiers were. On shore leave, any competitive hostility between combat Navy and Marines or Army was somebody's movie time myth. The soldiers knew well who scrambled out there at sea to improve their odds, and they showed their gratitude, not rivalry.

"'Heads-up, ladies,' snapped the deck officer, as I relieved the prior specialist at his duty station. In the morning light, a whiff of exploded air from the shore pounding overnight still hung over the waves. The *Waddell* held a steady, aggressive velocity while tacking westward toward the river's mouth. 'Captain will be announcing our release by Operations Tactical Command (OTC) this morning. We will be heading to the north Tonkin Gulf to conduct Sea Dragon patrols.'

"The daily acts of faith during wartime taken by soldiers and sailors alike on the front line are generally overlooked. Early on, I had figured out that it would be a waste of time to ask why the *Waddell* would be drawn away from one entirely fluid situation to another. My team was one cog in the overarching machinery of war. I could only hope that naval OTC was staffed by a clear-eyed and steady-handed team like the crew of the *Waddell* itself.

"Enemy supplies and personnel mostly flowed southward via a branching network of easterly backwoods paths known unlovingly as the Ho Chi Minh Trail. The system snaked resiliently through patches of Laos, Cambodia, and Vietnam. Bombing the hell out of one of its arteries all but assured that another passage would sprout almost immediately. North Vietnam's assets didn't include a bona fide Navy, although there existed a cadre of fast Chinese-made Swatow boats to defend North Vietnamese Army (NVA) troop and equipment infiltration both seaside and along coastal inland waterways.

"Only a few hours after emerging from the mouth of the Cua Viet, the CIC of *Waddell* was already coordinating with the USS *Cunningham* (DD752) and USS *Cogswell* (DD651) shooting up ample shore targets just north of the DMZ near Dong Hoi and Vinh Linh, both NVA staging areas. Harassment fire rained on radar sites, artillery, troop concentrations, ammunition storage, and anything else identifiable, or not.

"Nature ignores men's wars. Yet it's always an unwitting accomplice. The drizzly, winter monsoon preceded a roll back of the low cloud blanket, teasing us on some days with a few hours of clear sky. On those opportune days, the prop-driven Navy A-1 Skyraiders and Army O-1 Bird Dogs could better spot targets, and Combat Air Patrol could provide some protection for ships.

"The afternoon of April 1, 1967, wasn't one of those days. Beset by light rain and fog limiting visibility to 500 yards, the *Waddell* and the *Cunningham* zig-zagged into the path of the enemy waiting for us at the mouth of a small tributary near Tho Ngoa north of Don Hoi. Our objective was to fire on assets identified earlier by reconnaissance aircraft. I stayed glued to my surface radar screen, keen to distinguish waterborne craft from shore elements, a task made dicier by the weather's cluttering effects. What looked initially like a nondescript signal blip behind a jetty suddenly atomized into seven fast-moving craft advancing from the harbor toward the *Waddell*.

"'Chief, have six to seven probable torpedo boats,' I shouted out, 'now bearing on our passage at high speed. Fishing vessels unlikely.'

"'Roger that.' The Chief Petty Officer on deck quickly alerted the bridge via sound-powered phone. 'Keep a sharp eye, AJ. We're engaging.'

"The CPOs all looked the same to me in many ways. Thirty-five to forty years old already seemed a bit old and stodgy. Uniforms were tidy yet well-worn and betrayed a bit of spread in belly and butt. To the CIC team, the chief was leader, coach, big brother, and would take your head off if you weren't one hundred percent sharp in critical moments.

"As the fast-moving torpedo boats were rapidly closing the 9000 yards distance, *Waddell* fired one five-inch fifty-four-centimeter round at the leading three craft. The CPO's voice remained calm as he peered over my shoulder, stroking the day's chin stubble with a bit more vigor. He was well aware that the fog and rain thwarted any assistance from combat air patrol to defend the *Waddell* or to track the Swatow boats bearing down on us.

"'How blind are we, AJ?' he asked. 'Can you follow them at all?'

"'Chief, the pack is a bit of a blur,' I pointed him to the cluster on the screen, 'but the ping of that first shell showed up on surface radar, crystal-clear. If we lob shells in sequence, the pings may help. Put me on phone with the gunner's mate on mount 51, and maintain course, Chief.'

"The gift on the radar signal as the rounds splashed the surface would guide us in, walking the *Waddell*'s fire toward those ballsy attackers. On the screen, I would pace off the distance, accounting for speed of closure by the seat of my pants, and conveyed distance and line of launch to the gunner's mate, referencing degrees of port.

"'Connolly, are you calling these shots blind?' the chief snapped. 'What the fuck! Bridge says they can't see anything but a little glow off starboard.'

"Almost immediately, the leading three craft dissolved off the radar. I rolled my seat back at an angle and tapped at the diminished cluster for the chief to see. I didn't say anything presumptuous, but the chief got it immediately.

Four remaining craft were seen turning about for the tributary. 'Chief,' I said, 'we're not as blind as they think. Suggest maintaining course and pursuit.'

"As the *Waddell* advanced, the Swatow swift boat crews made the fatal error of assuming they were hidden behind a jetty. The *Waddell* continued to walk the five-inch fifty-four-centimeter rounds on the craft until all but one had disappeared. The seventh melted into the shoreline somewhere further up the tributary. We continued steadily up the tributary marking the targets identified here and there by the Skyraiders and Bird Dogs without being confronted again that shift.

"The chief stood close by but kept his eyes on the marked-up grease board that illuminated the battle area in the subdued light of the CIC. He spoke just loud enough to embarrass me in front of the crew. 'In my time, AJ, I've never seen it done quite that way. That was a nice piece of work. Glad I didn't rattle you. You may have just saved all our sorry butts. But don't go getting a big head, because you're still the lowest piece of shit in this man's Navy.' He got all that out without cracking a smile. It was the chief's way and strangely reaffirming to all of us. I must have been twenty, I think, at the time.

"For the next forty-eight hours, the *Waddell* continued shore fire and interdiction of unidentified southbound craft, and eventually laid in with the USS *O'Brien* and USS *Canberra* whose CO was the senior-officer-presently-afloat for the trio. This special operations group went dead on all emitting electronics—no radios, no radar, and no emitting-type fire control. We reached deep into the north of Tonkin between Hainan Island and the North Vietnamese mainland—a first time for me, and not to be the last. It was no secret that Hainan Island, though Chinese territory, housed Russian shore batteries and aircraft in defensive support to the Ho Chi Minh regime. Going dead had become routine in this arena, rendering US vessels less readily detectable, although we were not entirely invisible to these installations. Feedback from electronic counter measures indicated that the enemy was tracking the trio as it moved up the coast into the mouth of the Song Ma River. The Thanh Hoa Bridge over the Song Ma, known as the "Dragon Jaws," remained a sensitive pinch point for all goods flowing from north to south. As we set deeper into that wide and deep river, the morning skies were beginning to fill with fighter aircraft and bombers to bring the Thanh Hoa Bridge down.

"'Okay, ladies, stay sharp. This is the shit I don't particularly care for,' the chief started, as he hung up the line from the Waddle's CO. 'We are to continue hammering shore batteries while zig-zagging and provide search and rescue for any of our guys that get hit while bombing the bridge and other installations. If hit, they will attempt to skedaddle back to blue water or ditch into the river. As you know, our recon pilots make their live runs from inland eastward in the hopes that they'll get to our water if they are brought down. You know the drill. These jokers on either side of the shore artillery luckily don't seem to be able to hit shit!' he chuckled nervously. He knew they didn't have to be sharp-shooters, however, when employing air-burst rounds that detonated twenty-five to thirty feet above the ship and sprayed shrapnel everywhere.

"The *Waddell* would lick its wounds that day. While retrieving a Navy A-1 Corsair aviator from just north of the Song Ma estuary, one of those bursts left nine holes in the *Waddell's* metal just aft of the bridge and CIC with a related casualty.

"'Hey, AJ,' the gunner's mate popped his head in around the starboard doorway, as he passed the CIC en route to the mess kitchen. By then, the *Waddell* had already disengaged, having new orders directing her south once again. 'Hey, cowboy, didn't I see you having a smoke with Grable a couple weeks ago—you know the signalman?'

"'Hey, yourself, meathead!' I shouted back. 'Listen, if you're headed for chow, I'll catch up with you in about five minutes. Yeah, what about Grable?'

"The gunner's mate paused, leaned into the CIC, and slowly swept the other faces in the unit that were turning, one-by-one, to hear. He stepped forward, licked his lips, and looked straight at me, hands on his hips. So I'm half ignoring him, until I caught his face. The gunner's eyes darted nervously to the other faces again, and back to me.

"'Uh, were you guys close? Um, I guess you didn't hear.' Another pause. The 'were' had already said it all. Later, some guys told me I went pale; I don't remember that.

"The gunner continued slowly. 'Shit, man, he's gone. That air burst that hit during the last rescue? Grable was involved and got the guy out but took a chunk himself in the back of the head. Sorry, AJ, he was gone before they could get him to sick bay.'

"'No. I didn't know him well. I hadn't heard. Thanks, I'll see you at mess deck,' was all I could think to say.

"It was true. Yeah, I knew Grable . . . but really didn't. I don't know why his getting killed that way hit me so hard. I still don't. Anyway, I skipped the chow and just got some shut-eye. Grable and I had just had a smoke. I don't remember anything we said, if we said anything at all. Only reason I can think for me taking his loss hard was that he seemed just like me. Ship's log confirmed Grable was credited as instrumental in the pilot's recovery. It is what it is—an all-too-common conflict zone trade-off of one life for another. And there's always the 'why him; why not me,' shit. Sometimes I think I see his face in a crowd, still a kid, like I was."

Miko quietly extended the box of tissues, keeping silent in honor of the memory. Intellectualizing with the battle details ultimately had not saved AJ's poise, caught off-guard by insuppressible sobs.

"What do you make of all that, Doc?" AJ asked, regaining his composure. Sorry for so much context to answer your question, you know, about losing someone I knew personally. I guess you can't really talk about a casualty like that, you know, a real person who got killed—nothing 'casual' about it. You can't do a fallen soldier or sailor justice if you don't tell the whole story. You asked, and I answered the best I could, mostly from what I wrote for the *Waddell* website. Nobody expects you to cry forever over a killed shipmate. But I think it's part of our duty to remember them. Now, some fifty years later, I am honored to remember Billy Grable, even if no one else remembers the poor son-of-a-bitch. I should tell someone about his dedication and sacrifice. I'm glad you asked."

"What do I make of it, AJ?" Miko repeated. "If you don't feel that kind of loss, you are not human, or you've already shut down."

AJ wiped his face downward, pausing with brief finger pressure over the corners of his eyes. A sigh and heavy exhalation pacified his voice.

"Well, I admit it was confusing—the war and all," AJ posited.

Miko shuffled the chart, marked the appointment slip, then slid his pen into a breast pocket, and met AJ's eyes. "AJ, you're tackling powerful stuff. You've spoken of joy, a sense of purpose, accomplishment, and agility in the Navy. You've examined issues of fear and loss from the war—and all the emotions mixed-up with those. It's a lot! And it is confusing. After all this time, maybe you're beginning to sort it out."

Miko stood and rounded the desk and leaned back on the desk front. "Let's go to the next step. We'll schedule about four weeks from now. At that visit, I want us to zoom out a bit to look at a bigger picture. I think we may be ready to see if you have put your personal events into some broader context. Like, how were you thinking about the war then? Why you were there in the war? Have your views changed since that time? If so, how? Let me ask you to give it some thought until then."

CHAPTER 14

GRIM REALITY

The auditory contrast could not be starker and the message so much the same. Miko ruminated as his stride quickened with the end of the Angelus bells from Holy Family Cathedral across the street from the hospital. The Catholic equivalent of Islam's call to prayer could, in these days, be welcomed or abhorred in Tulsa. Either could remind Miko that he is late for his noon clinic's first patient.

Strange are the moments when self-doubt rears its head. From human physiology, anatomy, psychology to cardiovascular surgery, immunomodulatory infusions, and locked, padded inpatient areas for acute schizophrenics—what could the public possibly understand about the scope of knowledge expected of medical trainees, even within in a single specialty. His ultimate year of psych residency loomed just around the corner. In a palpable span of time, he would be expected to be a veritable master of the specialty. The thought made his heart pound. What had he taken on with no guarantee of success? Would he be yet another failure, masquerading effectiveness, and simply billing for his time? Would a writing career have provoked as much anxiety? Maybe not, he thought, but creative license rather than a medical license would be accompanied by a higher probability of destitution.

Luckily, the clinic had adopted a flag system so that the resident psychiatrists could navigate quickly to their next victims already roomed by the medical assistant. That gave Miko cover to be a couple of minutes late.

"You look busy! That's good." AJ chided, noting the slight glisten of sweat on Miko's brow as he whipped into the clinic room, unraveling scarf, gloves, hat, and long coat in a flurry.

"Sorry, AJ. Yes, it's never not busy here." Miko deflected. "Give me a moment to track back to where we are."

AJ pulled out a pocket-sized spiral note pad from the lapel pocket of his dated nylon shirt. "I did what you said, and since last visit, I've jotted some notes about what you asked; about what I thought of the war, if it makes any difference. I suppose you're wondering if all my faults came from war trauma, rather than me just being a drunk, mean, disorderly, wife-abusing asshole."

"Wife-abusing?" Miko responded, caught off-guard. "That's a strong implication. You implied before that your behavior made your wife unhappy. We started out to explore your military experiences and then your marriage that took place after. Is that still okay, or do you feel something else is more pressing?"

"No, no, that's fine; that's a good order, I think." AJ's mouth held tight so that another oops might not emerge.

"Okay." Miko's tone waffled with an element of uncertainty. "Then today, my plan was indeed to explore your thoughts on the bigger picture of the conflict in Vietnam and war in general. Let's develop some context for the war within the framework of the rest of your life, so to speak, in relation to the other rooms of your mind. Sometimes, it's hard to move forward with clarity without addressing the past."

AJ quickly passed Miko a few photos of himself, of the destroyer, of shipmates. Miko's attention caught on the black-and-white image of a young AJ, lean and muscular, standing at the stern taffrails, cropped hair tossed in a wild gust. The short sleeves of his dungaree shirt were rolled up, the smuggest of smirks drawn on his eyes and grin. Rough sea and menacing sky filled the background. No image could say it louder than this worn Kodachrome. AJ fit—the right time, the right place, no doubts.

Ψ

"A whole lot of us didn't have a clue about Vietnam when we entered the service. We heard about it, naturally, but it was just starting. For all we knew, our military presence would always just be advisors.

"By the time we were ready to go into action, we understood a lot more about it from general briefings. Didn't understand the scope, and we didn't care. Once there, we got indoctrinated quickly about how things work.

"Service men knew early on, nonetheless, we were wasting our time in Vietnam. We thought Army and Marine leaders were just wasting lives. We just said it, at least to each other and to our own CPOs and the like. We'd read the reports every day. We saw what was going on. Young soldiers would get killed taking this little village or that hill, and for what? Then we'd just give 'em up and leave; we never held territory. It just seemed pointless.

"You couldn't trust the South Vietnamese guys, the SVN; they skedaddled a lot. As they moved around the battlefield, they took their families with them. That was in the culture, and it was a big drawback. Some were good soldiers, but a lot were not well trained.

"In operations, I had a secret clearance and was able to see a lot of intelligence. We could tell early on Vietnam was not a winnable war. A big cause was the infighting among the leadership of SVN. There was a high-level assassination while I was there, the South Vietnamese president. Later the same month, our President Kennedy was assassinated. A lot of us started to wonder what the fuck was happening. We were assured that our command structure was still rock-solid, thank god, and that those killings were in no way related. In general, the SVN just were not capable nor motivated, and were corrupt. And we kept propping them up as though they were competent. We all had a feeling it wasn't right. The North Vietnamese Army had it together, especially while getting help from the Russians. They were more determined and had been for a lot of years before we got there. So the US sailor and the grunt in the field felt the whole engagement was a waste of time. The thing that kept us going were the other guys our age who depended on us.

"I served proudly; I just wish we could have won it. If you're not fighting to win absolutely, then stay the hell out of it.

"Navy has a versatility advantage where there are rivers; we are portable gunfire—easy-in and easy-out. We could go some ten miles upriver a lot of times. Picture this: these rivers are four to five miles wide and very deep. Take the Cue Vet River—a craft as big as a destroyer can easily go up and down it. Yet the Navy got little press because few reporters could come out and see what we were doing. If they tried, nine out of ten journalists got so seasick, we'd have to lift their asses off. So most folks only heard about the war in the trenches.

"About the whole war in Vietnam, there's not one thing that sums it up, but people try to do that all the time. Vietnam was so fluid, changing every day. To older folks at home, it was just a temporary cluster fuck, a few years of death and political conflict in the US. To us young guys, it had been our whole life up to then. Still, we weren't into the politics. We were just doing our job, and we shouldn't have even been there.

"Yes, I had a taste of fear when our compartment locked down after the collision with *Brinkley Bass*. Other than that, young men like me, with their buddies, don't really know fear. We were too stupid to understand how fragile the whole thing was. I never had enough fear to act from it. As a sailor, you know death is there, but you never felt it up close. You knew you could die the next day, but it's not an everyday thought.

"When your tour is over, sure, you are glad to get home. You ask yourself, 'Why did I get out of this shit, and another poor sucker got shot?' Like goddamn Greg Arthur who took it in the chest. You don't want to trade places, for sure, but it's like you didn't give equally at the till. His family is going to be sad and tore up. I don't have a scratch; my momma and daddy are happy. You feel the unfairness, especially if you know you're an asshole, and don't deserve the break you got.

"The usual reasons vets are angry don't seem to apply as much to me. I really can't put a finger on why I'm not right. Not the loss of friend so much, strangely enough—I think I have that in perspective—I can mourn and let go. Not the politics—I read enough history to put that in perspective. Who knows, if I hadn't gone, I may have been wondering about our military, its morals and capability. People can talk-talk-talk and get themselves into a group think, almost to a frenzy, and forget that these young guys were just trying to do their duty and survive. It's not the lack of appreciation, although at times, I admit, it would be nice to feel like the hero to my wife and kids, just a little.

"I have to laugh at myself and all of us vets who have tried to record the stories of our experiences on a ship's or a unit's website somewhere, as I have. We know nobody's going to read our stories except us—not even our kids. With the passing of our generation, all that bravado and history will evaporate like it never happened. All those ships have been decommissioned for decades. You go back and look at pictures of your buddies—jeez, they look like babies. A week before, we couldn't wipe our noses, and next week we were out there killing people. But I can live all that down. Maybe that's something I suppress; I considered that. That's why I'm still seeing you, Doc!"

"We've covered my notes well enough. Now, it seems kind of confused in the telling." AJ concluded, slipping the small pad back into the pocket.

"Not at all, AJ." Miko affirmed. "Granted, I've heard parts of this from other veterans in our program here—mostly the survivor guilt. Maybe we'll find something in your story that will enlighten all of us. Never sell yourself short. At the minimum, you fought loyally on your country's behalf."

"Loyalty was not so much to country, but to the guys and to the ship. You'd meet guys from different parts of the country, maybe black or Asian, American Indians; maybe from big cities or small, rural farm towns—whatever. At first you might find some of them to be really fucking weird, sometimes a sissy or a braggart, or have weird body movements. It didn't take long for all those weird things to just seem normal and that you'd fight as hard for that once-weird dude as anybody else.

"And the ship, well, she was our home. Think about it— for months, that island with an engine was our home, more than your home back in the States. People make comedy about the poor sailor swabbing the decks all the time or scrubbing the latrines. It didn't take long for any of us to figure out that our moms weren't there. That tank would go all to shit if we were not all cleaning it up and keeping things in working order. I knew guys who got kind of particular—you might say compulsive—about the cleanliness and orderliness, especially the ranking petty officers. For me, the chores got to be kind of a stress release when you had a chance to turn away from the battles and the rescues to more mundane shit, so you kind of looked forward to it."

"Now there's a mental adaptation, I'd say!" Miko scrunched his nose. "How common do you think that feeling about the ship was among your shipmates?"

"Yeah, I don't know . . . maybe not common." AJ acknowledged, his voice fatiguing from the exchange. "There was plenty of turn-over of crew during my three to four years on the *Waddell*, but, don't forget, I got her new. We got her ready for duty, and, well, it's like she and I hung together through the whole shitshow from there on out. Inseparable—maybe she became part of my identity. You get to where a ship becomes more of an animate object; like it grudgingly cares for you. Stern attitude, but she takes care of you, you know, like a good momma. And if you grumble about chores, you'll know from momma that it's got to be done. It's hard to explain, I guess, in human terms."

Miko was half-listening and passed AJ the slip for his next visit. "You already know that I want to get to the mental room about your marriage. We talked briefly before about how you and Natalia met, and how long you've been together. Let's get back to when you came home from the war and went on to marry and have your family. Then, I'd like to invite Natalia here to gather her perspectives.

"Whatever. Chances are you may not like much what she's got to say," AJ framed.

"Not my role to like or dislike, AJ." Miko reframed. "I'm on the side of getting you to a better place. I suspect Natalia will be a big part of that, one way or another."

CHAPTER 15
RUSH TO MARRY

Entering the office door, AJ was wrapping up the refuse of the MacDonald's meal he had grabbed on his way in. It occurred to Miko for the first time that he had never seen AJ wearing any lingering signs of a military past, like a bit of khaki, or the cap or vest emblazoned with unit or campaign awards that other vets never leave home without. Miko understood the ritual broadcasting to comrades and anyone who would take notice, and made note of AJ's avoidance of the practice. Maybe the department could find a grant, he pondered, for an exploratory study of those who did and those who did not.

"Sorry, Doc." AJ smeared the last blot of mayo from a corner of his mouth. "I had to grab a bite on my way, and it almost made me late."

"No worries, AJ." Miko opened the chart, slipped off his white coat and hung it over the back of the desk chair. "Let's get started. You were going to tell me about how things developed with you and Natalia when you got home from your active duty. I understood that it had become a fixture in your mind that you two would get married, work, and have kids, and life would be great. And you ran into some unexpected feelings. Help me understand those things."

Ψ

"Well, one Friday evening, maybe a couple of months after I got home from active duty, I was exhausted after a week at McDonnell Douglas Aviation, the first job I could get, working on aircraft wing construction. I was starving, so we decided to go out to the Pines Drive-in, a burger place where we used to go when we were dating before I left. We were driving Natalia's yellow and black Malibu her parents had bought her.

"'Holy cow! Natalia, is that Jamie with you?' Rita called from the passenger seat as the new, two-tone '69 Cutlass 442 swung into the next slot. Rita was with her boyfriend. 'You remember my fiancé, Bobby, right?' Natalia's friends almost needed to shout over their own car radio to be heard, which was annoying to me.

"'Hey Rita. Hi, Bobby. Yep, AJ's been back from the Navy for a few weeks.' Natalia leaned back so I could look over to the car on the right. Hell, I just wanted to eat my cheeseburger and slid down a bit in the seat. 'Say hi, AJ!' Natalia said, to get me out of my antisocial attitude. 'Everybody calls him AJ since he's home 'cause that's what they called him in the Navy. How are you guys?'

"'Hey, Jamie, are you home for good?' Rita shouted, lowering the radio as Bobby simultaneously shut the car off.

"'I'm in the reserves for another two years but probably done with any more active duty. How are you guys?' They looked a bit familiar, but these encounters happened almost every day, where Natalia would run into one of her friends from high school or church, and the same conversation would take place. Seemed like she knew everybody, and I didn't want to know any of them.

"'Bet you're glad to be out, huh, AJ.' Bobby called out. 'That's a mess over there. My draft number was in the middle of the lottery, but going to the junior college got me a deferment.'

"'Well, it's good to be back, but, strange as it may sound, I miss it a little. My ship was pretty active and successful in the fight, particularly during interdiction efforts in the north.'

"Natalia looked at me with a little smile and turned back to her friends. 'What have you guys been up to?' She deflected.

"'Believe it or not, we might get tickets to the Beach Boys concert next month at the civic center. You guys want to come along?'

"'Wow, that sounds exciting, but probably not. We're saving money for the wedding and down-payment on a house. Anyway, AJ mostly likes different stuff like James Brown and Roy Orbison.'

"Natalia could guide the chatter away from anything serious so deftly around her friends, I stopped bringing up the war or anything that I had been doing. We'd have parties once in a while after we got married, some with family and friends, and it would all be the same kind of stuff. Mostly, when my brothers got back home, I'd go out with them. Greg got to be a homebody of sorts with a bit of a nagging wife. So then it was usually me and Mike.

"At the aircraft plant, I helped an electrician on some projects, and he got me interested in electrical as a career. So I went to night school for two years and apprenticed at St. Francis Hospital to get licensed. Thank god for that. I would spend the next thirty years there, quickly rising to run the whole department. I was hungry—hungry for a challenge, hungry to be around serious people. I sure wasn't getting that at home. Natalia was interested in what people were wearing, nice things for the house, going shopping with her mother, all that stuff. Back then, she might have a part-time job here and there at a department store, and then with preschool kids. Her jobs didn't pay much. She never got any training for a skill. I guess I got resentful that I had all the responsibility, and I took it out on her. When the kids came along, well, that kept us together and kept us apart, I guess. We both worked at the relationship, probably her more than me, and I doubt either of us knew how to do it well. We'd have good times alright, but harbored resentments; me for her not seeming to deal with bigger issues, and she for my temper, especially when I'd been drinking. It really bothered her, even though I never thought it was that bad. No doubt, everyone knew I was peeved about something, and she'd get the worst of it."

Ψ

"Communication would seem like such a natural thing," Miko began his closing sermon for the visit. "But when problems continue, it's common that we are just not communicating well. We know better what we mean to say than how it is received. And we filter what we hear through our own set of values and experiences so much that we often miss the point. In that case, couples can go for years, maybe forever, talking past each other. Marriage counselors, who are the social workers helping with couples' issues, are mainly skilled in getting the parties to learn active listening; to think about what they want to communicate before talking, before the other person's listening window closes. Have you two ever sought counseling for the marriage?"

"No." AJ responded, definitively. "Well, she has. She's gone by herself. Still does from time to time. But it escapes me how a stranger could tell us how to get along when we're the ones living together. So, no, I—we haven't gone to counseling. That bugs her, too. Hope you're not going to suggest that, Doc!"

"I may suggest a lot of things at one point or another, AJ, if there's reason to think it may be helpful." Miko showed no surprise at the resistance and didn't roll over. "It would make more sense, first, for me to get some viewpoints from your wife, if she's willing and you have no objection. Can I have the staff set up a visit with Natalia?"

"Sure, go ahead. She'll probably give you an ear full. She's likes to talk and is not shy about raking me over the coals." AJ paused. "I'm assuming you don't want me there, so she might be more candid."

"Yes, that's the general idea, in the beginning. There may come a time and a setting when both of you will come together, either with me or a counselor, so be open to that." Miko held up a reminder slip for AJ's next appointment, rocking back in the desk chair before handing it over. "You know, AJ, going into the marriage room almost seems to make you more uncomfortable than going into the wartime room. Or is it just that wartime is in the past, and this is now?"

AJ smirked, nodding wordlessly to the side, and shrugged.

"Anyway," Miko concluded as he rose, "You're still here. That's a good sign. I think we'll get through any tough parts, and you may be better off for it. Keep the faith!"

CHAPTER 16

UNTOLD

Natalia rose from the chair to greet Miko as he entered the office. "Nice to meet you, finally, Doctor! I'm Mrs. Connolly, AJ's wife. You can call me Natalia, even though I'm probably more than twice your age," Natalia giggled, extending a handshake to Miko. Returning to her seat in front of the desk, she tugged at the bottom of her yellow cotton-knit sweater and straightened the shirttail exposed below it. She had taken note of the room's aged trappings before Miko had arrived, noting the cleanliness despite the worn motif of the stately building—a bit charming, and less drab than the ward where she had visited AJ once during his mandatory stay of admission.

"And you can call me Doctor or Miko, whatever is more comfortable for you." Miko was accustomed to the quip about his relative youth from patients and family members. "Thank you for coming in, Natalia. As you know, AJ and I are trying to work through some issues that might be of use to both of you. How would you feel about that?"

"Well, I have to admit, we're not the types who would ordinarily go to a psychiatrist." Natalia leaned in with a low voice, avoiding eye contact. "People just work things out or they don't, I guess. But if the Public Health or VA is paying for this, then I guess I'm for it. It probably can't hurt." Miko kept silent as he watched Natalia's smile slip away to pursed lips, and her voice hush to a near whisper. "I need to admit another thing before you get started. I'm in Al-Anon, you know, for people who live with an alcoholic. My counselor there says I'm more sick than AJ because I stay with him and keep taking the abuse. I know she's right," Natalia's voice cracking as she nervously covered her mouth. "Sorry," she continued. "I'm sure you're busy, so I won't beat around the bush. I think I understand why you brought me here."

Miko sat up, noting her beeline from the small talk, surmising her time with an Al-Anon counselor had conditioned her to the therapeutic environment. "Thank you for sharing that." Miko was ready to take advantage of Natalia's nervous push of speech, and let it flow. "Al-Anon is a good organization. And since we're there already, I'll ask you to tell me about any abuse, and if it is continuing. Then, with our time, I'll ask you to give me the general picture of your life together and how things have developed."

Natalia sat back in the chair, elbows on the arms, palms elevated from there, pausing there before beginning. "Well, long story short, it started almost immediately after we were married. He'd just criticize me and cut me down until I felt like nothing and worthless. Then, as his drinking got worse, it got to be gradually more physical with slapping and shaking. Later, there was some marital rape that happened. Now that we're older and the kids are out, it's not physical anymore, thank god. He stopped smoking and has cut back on drinking since his heart bypass, but he still sneak-drinks and lies to my face about it. We are both in the same house, and we try to be civil. I do my best to just avoid him most of the time."

Miko disguised his surprise at the clarity and brevity with which this slight, casual lady had delivered an account that usually would require careful exploratory questioning over weeks. He retreated to formulaic affirmation. "That sounds incredibly hard to endure. I'm glad you've reached out to Al-Anon. It has a good track record helping people victimized by alcoholism or other substance abuse. Of course, you may know well the fog of living with a partner with the disease of addiction. I want to come back to your experiences with that in more detail." Miko rolled in his office chair around to the side of the desk, positioning comfortably perpendicular to Natalia's chair with a seat that could swallow two copies of her thin frame. Physically shifting when he redirected the conversation had become an unconscious technique. "It's easy to admire and yet to be puzzled why someone stays in those circumstances, as they often do. The reasons are usually not so simple. To understand, it would help me to get a picture of how you two got together in the first place, maybe in happier times. Can you talk about that?"

Natalia lifted her face, and her eyes followed from the floor. Miko leaned forward, elbows on the chair arms, and crossed his knees, broadcasting his listening mode. Natalia's smile gradually resurfaced.

"Well, I know there are things in my personality that make me a sucker for someone like Jamie—that's what some of us who knew AJ before the Navy still call him sometimes. I was raised by an Italian mother who was a war bride. Long and short, she hated being in America and forever blamed my dad for her misery. Poppo was pretty submissive, constantly trying every way he could to make her happy. After she had her third child at twenty-four, she hemorrhaged and had a hysterectomy, followed by a nervous breakdown, or whatever you call it nowadays. Anyway, she went into a psychiatric hospital and had shock treatments, saw doctors, and was on Valium for a very long time. Mom remained cruel to Dad; I tried to protect him, since he would never defend himself. He adored her, even after she would throw pots and pans at him. He was always a pleaser, and I guess I got that from him. It sort of became my job to take care of both of them, Momma and Poppo, as well as my two little brothers. Both boys will have nothing to do with Mom now, since they've grown up. They still remember how she would get a branch off a tree and switch their bare legs viciously. Even after I got married, I never went shopping without bringing my parents with me to get them out of the house. Mom thought that was my job. They became like children to me, constantly needing my attention until Poppo died at ninety-one, and Mom went into the care home with mobility problems. AJ was pretty supportive, when he wasn't drinking, especially while his own folks were alive; he was good to them, too. He was generally good that way, but he would certainly not have my Momma live in our home. That's where he drew the line.

"At the start, well, we were probably too young to be in a relationship, but that was common in our generation. There was not so much of a romance, but a courtship of sorts, you could say. I was the scraggly, skinny, little girl up the street. I only first noticed him when he hit me in the head with an ice ball one winter. Another time, Mom opened the door and let him in, and he dragged me outside in my pajamas and threw me into the snow. Kid stuff, I guess; his awkward way to show affection. I couldn't have been more than fifteen or sixteen.

"He always thought we would get married, even before the Navy. He somehow assumed I'd be waiting for him, but I wasn't that serious, and I never got there. We were different. And then, he and his dad had a fight, and he signed up into the Navy and was gone. The one time he came home on leave in four years, he was mad because I was dating someone else. When he finished his tour of duty, he was mad that I had dated other people while he was gone. But I wasn't with anyone at the time, and we started dating again. He just had a thing about me. I was on a pedestal. I was so young and naive. I may have fallen for the way he felt about me; he thought that I was so much more than I was. My vision was to marry someone who wanted what I wanted—kids and a peaceful life. I thought once we were married, it would all come together; he just needs a home and someone to care. I thought like so many women who were wrong. I didn't really know what he was like until after we got married. He was a monster. His behavior changed suddenly the day we got married. He looked at me as someone he had to support, and all of a sudden, he thought he had to feel guilty if he couldn't do it first class. Well, feeling guilty just is not in his DNA. He knew I was good to him, but it seemed beyond him to just be good to me. His checklist was that a good wife keeps house spotlessly, cooks good meals every night, and keeps up the yard. It became a competition of who was doing the most work, and I better not be doing less than him, because he was out working and making the living, so I better be doing as much in other ways.

"He blamed me and everyone else for having to fight in an ugly war that made no sense, and for not being appreciated. He has probably been depressed his whole life and full of hate. I found out his dad had treated his mom in the same way, only for me, the browbeating was a thousand times worse."

Miko sat spellbound by the images she wove, and the intentionality she showed to not squander an opportunity to say these things aloud. So many other women, living the same way, remain silent.

"Well, for instance, one night, a Saturday, during my middle pregnancy, AJ had dropped me at my parents' house to go out drinking with his friends. When I slipped in through Momma's narrowly-opened screen door dragging my two-year-old behind me, I almost missed Momma waving off AJ in his car, using the back of her hand swiped under her chin; and, of course, AJ returned the salute with a middle finger. Those hand gestures sort of mean the same thing from different countries.

"'That boy is crazy and you know it!' Momma said. She wasted no time launching into a litany of AJ's faults. 'Why does he bring you here again on Saturday night. Doesn't he drink enough during the week? Why did you get pregnant again with him. You're more crazy than he is. He won't be a papa, he's still not grown up himself!' I didn't need to hear it again.

"Poppo didn't say anything, as usual, and kept his eyes on the television screen. He and I both knew you can't answer Momma's tirades. We were just hoping we'd get through a movie before AJ would return, probably drunk, and then we'd all keep quiet so as not to spark his anger.

"She'd ask 'Why doesn't he take you out anyway? Why does he bring you over here?' Natalia mimicked her mother's gesticulations, hands on her hips.

"I said, "Momma, he likes to see his friends, who like to drink. I don't like to drink and that aggravates him. Since I'm pregnant, I can't drink anyway, so he sees no point in taking me out. Anyway, all they ever talk about is work or the service. I never have anything to say. So I'd rather be with you and Poppo, okay?"

"'Shew!' Momma shook her head. 'Good thing you've got us and don't have to be with a crazy man all the time. Why don't you make us some popcorn before the movie starts?'

"But you know, as much as I hated getting that from her, I am grateful I had them at times like those. You know—someone on my side, some acknowledgment that this wasn't normal, and that it was not all just me. Anyway, I fell asleep on the couch during an old Bing Crosby and Gene Kelly musical with my little boy curled-up asleep on the floor. It really was a rest from a week of navigating the minefield of living with AJ. I could relax for a little while, you know, away from his bursts of anger over any wrong step or word.

"But that would end like it started. About three hours later, the honking sent Poppo into a quick step to turn on the porch lamps and to peer through the window to see what state of sobriety AJ was in. I woke up startled, and I could feel my heart beating fast in my chest and in my big belly. It was a drizzly night. The dim porch light and the one corner streetlight showed the rain bouncing in the street. AJ honked again, a long honk, so you knew he was in a mood, but you couldn't see into the car. I could just feel what was coming. Poppo's worried look broke my heart. He wasn't someone who could confront AJ by then, and he'd always hope that there wouldn't be a shouting match on the front steps.

"'The baby's asleep,' Poppo muttered, while I hustled to get my things together. 'Just leave him here with us, and we'll bring him to you at Mass in the morning.'

"So I ran out in the rain with my jacket overhead and got into the front seat without a word, and barely able to get the car door shut before AJ sped off in a wild, 180-degree turn-about, and off we went.

"The smell of sweat, alcohol, and cigarette smoke almost knocked me over. AJ was brooding and restless. I just looked away through my window; I knew just looking at him, even if lovingly, could piss him off. Out of the corner of my eye, I saw him cock his right arm and I turned my head turned away. But that slap knocked both contact lenses out, and my head smacked my side window.

" 'Jamie, please don't!' I begged, knowing it wouldn't matter.

"'You goddamn worthless bitch. I don't know who's more stupid—you, or me for marrying someone so useless!' AJ went on, as usual.

"'Can we please just go home?' I begged again. I was crying and sweating myself, but at least there were no bleeding cuts on my head and the window hadn't cracked. I could have done the same old rant for him—how hard he works while I do nothing to help out; how I'm still such a stupid teenybopper, like all the other piss-ants who don't know shit about the war or hard work. 'When are you going to grow up?' was the point he would usually pause to catch his breath.

"The hair grabbing and smacks to the back of the head were jarring but left no marks. Guarding my face with my arms would leave less to explain. I wondered, was it the rain, the bursts of wind? Was it the lightning that threw him into these rages? He was recklessly careening down wet country roads on the outskirts of town. You could barely see the road in front of you; everything else was black.

"One night during my first pregnancy, pretty much like the second, he had slowed down at a railroad crossing with the lights just beginning to flash. I sensed that he was about to drive around the railroad crossing boom to kill us both, so I bolted, leaving the car door wide open. Well, he chased and caught me and dragged me screaming in the dark back toward the flashing lights. The signal gong was drowned out by the freight cars blasting by. The cold of the rain, the rain pounding the car, the windshield wipers beating, and the high beams flashing back off the passing rail cars all seemed to wake him just enough from his death wish for us to survive.

"This last time, though, felt different. I could no longer hear my own screams. Nothing amid the engine noise, the grinding road, or the storm seemed to settle him down. I thought that would be the night my unborn child would die with us in a crash and a fire. But somehow, we got home. Those angry bulging eyes just gradually faded to dead and empty while he was trying to light another cigarette.

"When I got home from Sunday morning Mass, I avoided the bedroom where he was sleeping and kept to the kitchen, knowing he would expect to find me ready for whatever he wanted. I could hear the cough and nose blowing through the din of the shower. It seems that he could wash the stink away from himself, right along with any responsibility, remorse, or recollection.

"'Good breakfast, Natalia,' he said, when he took a moment away from the TV news shows. 'Any more bacon?'

"I tried to get him to think while he was still spent. I said, 'Jamie, you scared me to death last night. You can't be driving like that when you've been drinking. You'll get us both killed. You have people depending on you.'

"And you know what he said? He said, 'I know. You're right. It won't happen again, so just let it go.'"

"How have the children fared, Natalia?" Miko asked softly.

"You know, I kept telling myself—I guess kidding myself—that I should stay with him. The kids really seem to love him; a lot has faded for them. It's the same old BS I hear at Al-Anon—when he's sober, he's fun with the kids and grandkids, interested in what and how they're doing, and I think they feel that. They hate it when he drinks. But now, I'm talking like they're still kids—they're not. They are grown and gone and have made their own peace of sorts. They learned to hide when he got mean and just stayed out of his way. It was confusing and sad for them, but he's the only dad they've got. They wish that their parents got along better; they see that it's not good. Everyone has adapted in his or her own way. I'm so grateful, that it was just yelling, and he never once hurt them—something in his head says it's okay to slap your wife around, but it's not okay to hurt a child. Go figure! Anyway, I'm deeply grateful it's that way for the kids, as one might say—a separate peace." Natalia drew a breath to say more and stopped. She smiled at Miko. "I'm grateful that you asked, Doctor. I'm grateful that you asked, well, about all of it."

"You're welcome." Miko nodded.

She pulled the small purse sitting beside her to her lap. "I guess this is like a confessional, and you're like a priest—everything is confidential, right? Without the other spouse present, you don't tell them what's been said."

"Very much like that," Miko confirmed, "under these circumstances."

Miko held the quiet between them; the storm now passed, like thunder and lightning with no rainfall, spent with no reward.

"You'll let me know if you need me to do anything else, I'm sure."

"Yes." Miko replied. "I'm going to ask you to be aware for your own safety going forward, even if you think he has mellowed some. You are aware of the circumstances of his previous hospitalization—that he was found with a gun."

"I'm much safer now than I once was, and I don't worry about it. The damage is done. I have no skin scars to show for it. I guess some people would say the 'hot war' between us is over. I'm pretty religious—Catholic—and divorce would feel like failure to me still, like I had quit somehow. But I can't say that I'm not deeply disappointed." Straightening herself and the already orderly shirttails and sweater, she rearranged her public smile.

Miko heard Natalia's words, and saw hopeful eyes, notwithstanding.

The graceful woman extended both hands in farewell. "You seem like an excellent young psychiatrist, but I don't expect much to change. AJ is the only one who can change himself. Despite him being dragged in here, and the fact that he is still talking to you—as unlikely as that is already—I don't think he's ready, and odds are he never will be. I'm not saying miracles can't happen, but I'm getting older, and not sure how much I care anymore. What happens will be his own doing. Or maybe I'll go live with one of the kids someday."

CHAPTER 17
13,200 VOLT HIGH

An early spring taunted with a balmy ambiance, ahead of the humidity to begin anew with May's flowering. Buds threatened to burst into leaves overnight. Tepid breezes stroked the limbering elms in a mesmerizing hush. Winter would depart with a string of gentle morning showers. Most would forget for the rest of the year that it was ever this luxurious in Oklahoma. Miko continued to relish the internal domain his walks to work allowed amid the exotic distinctions here from Vathi. He would try to hold onto his own simple adventure as life pushed him forward.

"So you called in yesterday and asked for this earlier appointment? What's up, AJ? You've never done that before, as I recall." Miko mimicked the sarcasm he'd seen from AJ in their many chats. "I always got the sense that you thought you were doing me a favor by showing up for our sessions. Now you are asking to see me?"

"Two days ago, I had a fucked-up day." AJ started, dismissing Miko's leveling comment. "I thought that these sessions were calming me down, you know; that I was getting better at thinking first before blowing a fuse, even when I'd been drinking. But I'm not."

Miko, slid his chair toward the desk, putting on his professional face. "Tell me about two days ago. I can see you're upset. Start from the beginning."

"I knew you'd say that." AJ returned the sarcasm. "It's kind of a blur already, but I'll try. Something, I mean, well, something came to mind, an idea, you know. Maybe I stumbled into one of those rooms you talk about. At the time, it seemed kind of earthshaking, you know, like I'd figured something out. Now today, it doesn't seem like a big deal, like maybe it's just common sense, and I'm the only fuckstick who didn't get the memo."

"Okay, my friend, I'm listening. I want to hear the whole story. Slow down and just map out what happened as best you can." Miko encouraged again, leaning forward.

"Well, it's hard to explain. The team, all us electricians were gathered as usual for morning coffee or a bite in the cafeteria, you know, getting the report of events over night, and lining up the day's priorities. I got ticked-off at my pager, buzzing with the office extension number. I had just gotten off the same line with Millie, the office girl. I thought my instructions had been clear enough. PSO, the power service company for eastern Oklahoma, was to send someone over to check the main line into the hospital after two power fluctuations overnight. Millie kept paging. The aroma of the coffee was beyond great, and it's free to full-time staff. I just wanted to sit there, you know."

A bouncing knee belied his calm as AJ digressed. "Did I ever tell you that I stepped into the lead position of the hospital's electrical department at thirty-four years old? Now I'm the old dude on the young team we've assembled. I poached the best I could find from contract outfits who came in during area updates. All these guys are sharp, and I trust them. We've built a good work life, each pulling their weight—not like the finger-pointing, dog-eat-dog situations I'd been told about in the civilian world. There's a story around St. Francis about how one of my guys caused a major shutdown with a misplaced screwdriver, and I took the heat for it. Sister Blandine, the administrator, bragged about me, I'm told, in a talk to the executive staff on leadership."

"That's interesting, AJ, and let's come back to that another time," Miko redirected, taking note of the tangentiality not typical of previous conversations. "Just a moment; I want to do a doctor thing here." Miko interrupted, gently palpating AJ's pulse at the wrist, scrutinizing nail bed color, and noting the mild hand tremor. "I'd like you to concentrate on the events two days ago that got you here today. Can you do that?"

"Maybe I'll just walk you through it as I remember, and hope it'll make some sense. Millie, our department coordinator, said PSO wanted us to do an internal analysis before they'd send anyone out. They'd told her I should know what to look for. My guys already had their assignments for the morning, so I said I'd go to the central vault to check for issues. Before I could finish that good coffee, my assistant chief reminded me of my own protocol that no one enter the vault—what we call 'the beast'—alone, so he offered to tag along. I told him I was just planning to peer in. Unless there's something obvious, I'm just going to call PSO back. Hell, the crew had just done the weekly testing two days ago. There was no need for an assistant to follow.

"The beast lives in the sub-basement and houses cables bearing 13,200 volts that run from the PSO station into the hospital, as well as minivan-sized switches and transformers. I won't bore you with explaining all that. PSO wanted me to look for an inside problem that I knew we didn't have, before they'd come inspect for the outside problem I knew they'd find.

"When I headed for the sub-basement, the stairs on the way down seemed to sway a bit. The caffeine was working to clear some of the fog, yet the legs were lagging. I knew I should not be going to the vault alone. Point being, I've gotten good at lying to everyone, even better to myself. I was doing it to hide for a while. I had gotten bombed the night before and didn't get home until, I don't know, maybe two, two-thirty. Last I remembered, I was pissing out the side garage door, and then the damn alarm clock going off. I supposed I blacked out. Natalia had locked herself in the bathroom again. God only knows why.

"Anyway, when I got to the vault, I put a chair inside the first door, where I could sit and get just five minutes of shut-eye. It was then that I had some sort of crazy flashback, and not about the war. My mind just got flooded with shit; I couldn't think straight. I was afraid to move. I didn't know if I was having a stroke, a seizure, or could this be some kind of withdrawal. There was nobody around. And there I was in the 13.2 KV cable room. I just held on to the chair, closed my eyes, and listened to the buzzy silence. You talk about fear. I was thinking how much that placed seemed like a tomb—and maybe it would become my tomb. My skin tingled all over, you know, mouth dry, like taking cold shower when you're sleep deprived. It felt like the seat was moving underneath me.

"Anyway, after about a half an hour, things calmed down. I got out of the vault, took the elevator up, and called Millie that I was going home with a virus. I didn't go to the ER at St. Francis for obvious reasons, but I did go to my primary doctor's office yesterday morning. They'd had a cancellation and got me in. I told her about most of what had happened. She's an internist and aware of my heart issues. She looked me over pretty thoroughly, did an EKG, and took some blood and urine. She thought it was probably a panic attack and let me go home. I'm supposed to let her know if anything else happens."

AJ paused in a tense stare, breathing more labored, mouth open, as a man looking for an escape.

"And now you have come to my office today for a purpose, AJ." Miko calmly guided. "What more do you want to tell me?"

AJ's eyes widened, more pleading now, and turned slowly to Miko. "Doc, whatever the cause, my god, I thought I was doomed at that moment. And the, the, the evil that went through my mind . . . I knew I was going to hell. Just one bad memory after another. In my head, I saw a .357 magnum in my hand and slipping extra rounds into my pocket. It was the night Natalia had called my dad for help, who called the Tulsa police, who found me and had brought me in before I could waste some bullying bastard who had shown up like King Shit at Arnie's. I had shamed myself in front of my father. There I was, still the angry kid, still learning to live like a grown man in civilian life. Natalia and the kids didn't need this. I was torturing everyone I loved.

"In another flash, Natalia was shouting with her back to me, shielding one of the kids as a baby—'No Jamie, please, watch what you are doing!' she was saying. I was waving the magnum around in one hand, leaning for support on the doorjamb to the kid's bedroom with the other. 'Please put that away and let's go to bed,' she went on. 'Shut the fuck up, you whiny bitch!' I said to her. 'These are your goddamn kids. I never wanted this life!'

"Natalia hasn't told me what you two talked about; I don't blame her, Doc. Doubtful she told you the half of it. In the vault, I was sort of swaying on that chair, looking at this bad movie in my head. In another memory, there I was drunk again. I had grabbed Natalia by the hair and pulled her backward to our bedroom where I stripped her and slapped her out of any resistance. I glanced to the side and saw my own face in the mirror—bulging eyes, gritting teeth, dripping with sweat, like some ghoulish ape. She let out like a banshee, a scream that just petered off into whimpering sobs. Crazy thing—it reminded me of the sound of ships scraping into each other. I finished doing her as she just laid passive with her skinny arms wrapped around her face. I realized I'd done this many times before. When I was drunk, it felt good to see her cry and give in to me. Next morning, it would always be like it never happened—or she must be okay with it.

"While I sat there in the beast, at one point, I reached for the main 'off' breaker, something I'd do in testing the system. It was just an impulse. God knows what stopped me! If I had done that before initiating the backup—there are people on ventilators, pumps, and other life support in the hospital. Those suckers' survival depends more on me, in that building, than on their doctors.

"I'm sorry for rambling. I'll get to the point. When my head settled down and I felt some control coming back, it felt like someone or something was drawing me by the hand to take that goddamn metal chair and jam it in. That's all it would take. I could fry myself to a crisp in a second there, and I know exactly how to do it. I wasn't ready to take responsibility for those other deaths along with my own. So I mentally walked through the steps to initiate the backup generator before interrupting the main line for the conduction check. I stuck my free hand in one pocket, like a rookie, to avoid touching anything live without thinking. I finished the check successfully.

"A crazy thought hit me as I locked up and went for the elevator. There was no thrill to the danger anymore, not like when I was that Navy kid. For a moment, I missed that bigger feeling—out there in the open—like the bosun's chair back then. I remembered the minutes under water."

CHAPTER 18

BOSUN'S CHAIR

"**I** didn't want to interrupt, AJ," Miko broke in, "but what are you talking about, 'under water'? And what's a bosun's chair?"

"The bosun's chair may be the whole point of why I wanted to come today, Doc," AJ rubbed his face and ran the fingers of both hands through his scalp. "Guess I'm still having trouble getting to the point, again, huh?"

"It's okay. Go on," Miko hid his impatience imperfectly.

"The *Waddell* CO had called me up early in my shift one day to bring the Ticonderoga on station with the other carriers and destroyer escorts. Ticonderoga's CO had the conn and insisted on me. At nineteen or twenty, a mere petty officer third class, I was the most experienced sailor in the grouping at guiding formations. The bosun's chair was a high line, like what people call a zip line nowadays, to get an individual from one ship to another.

"It wasn't a big deal to me—putting ships on station with others—because a destroyer is lining up for something almost continuously—putting ourselves on station for refueling, getting supplies, getting ammunition, doing plane guard on a carrier—always fitting ourselves in somewhere. They had higher-ranking guys on the carriers that hadn't ever done it. So the next minute, I was launched in the chair over the water to the carrier in this cage that's not easy to escape.

"The seas were swelling to fifteen feet minimum, not ideal as you can imagine. Although downwind to the aircraft carrier Ticonderoga, southwest gusts provided a set of waves that, even with everyone on fixed bearings, a sudden reduction in the gap put enough slack in the line that I was submerged. That was freakishly uncommon for these transfers. I knew that I could be dragged under long enough to be drowned, or the cage could be bashed against the Ticonderoga's hull. I could be crushed if the vessels come into contact. A moment like that requires complete submission—faith that everyone would look out for me, and it would be alright—if it wasn't, at least I'd be dead quick. I had a job to do. My eyes closed. The wind went silent; muffled engine noise was all I could hear as I was dragged under. I can still feel it—that vulnerable moment of trust in others. Just when I thought my lungs would burst, I exploded out of the sea, as the line came taut again.

"They brought me aboard the Ticonderoga, and someone threw me a towel so I could get into the side seat with the conn. Couple of guys laughed; the CO just smiled as I approached, still dripping. I simply sat down and managed, as calmly as I'd ever been, to put three other carriers perfectly on station with the Ticonderoga, as well as three escort destroyers. The high-line back to the *Waddell* was uneventful, just in time for my four-hour break. And that was that. I couldn't have died a happier soul.

"Being department supervisor at the hospital, now, here I was again—the favored one to do the job. I realized that even still, with all the responsibilities of this "ship," it was a letdown after those Navy days. Was there any point in going on, if the best was already long past? It would have been so easy and so quick to end it there in the vault, like an accident, rather than purposeful. No one would know. No one would see me at my worst. So I guess I just jumpstarted myself again, at least this time . . ."

"AJ, are you still with me?" Miko's voice gently broke in among the thoughts. "I'm trying to follow, but it's not easy. You are going back and forth in time, place to place. I didn't want to interrupt your stream of consciousness. Maybe there's an opportunity for discovery here. But I need your help. What are we learning here today?"

"My worst tendencies are just under the surface. I'm like a good commander at work. Then I go drink a little and sometimes manage to do all kinds of awful things." AJ's voice trailed off in monotone. "I've gotten it more under control over the years, but it's still there. I may be the worst kind of coward—too big a pussy to kill myself, and too weak to change."

"That's pretty judgmental and self-loathing, AJ. How do you think all this gets us to a better place? You just said that you're good at work. That important room sounds tidy." Miko shifted in his chair. "This other room sounds like, well, what other vets would call, a 'clusterfuck.' Are you telling me you miss the war? What is it about the war and treating Natalia badly?"

"The war?" AJ's voice steadied. "Vietnam was the only time I wasn't at war with myself! I was a natural at that job, for the time, for the work to be done. Hell, it wasn't about the individual. It takes everyone to make it work, from the mess cook on up—the whole ship. And when we did that, it was pure magic. I was a puke third-class petty officer—it didn't matter. Anything you proved that you could do, they'd let you do—control combat aircraft at eighteen years old or coordinate gunfire support. I'd talk to spotters on the beach and in the aircraft, target and fire the guns, and wait for reports back on success or failure. I put the goddamn largest aircraft carrier formation in the world at the time on station. The challenges I had as a kid, you could never, ever get anywhere else. Ever! That built confidence!"

AJ caught himself out of breath, inhalations becoming halting. For the first time, he snatched a Kleenex from the cutesy box on Miko's desk, blew his nose and dried his eyes.

"I left the Navy because Natalia and I fell in love, or at least I did." AJ calmed himself, as if owing Miko some explanation. "Natalia has been an easy target to blame. My worst flashbacks, if that's what they were, have been about mistreating her in a fit of rage, rather than the war."

AJ rose from his chair, turned his back to Miko, and stared out the large windows with the metal frames, the lower row open to cool air. He ambled over to the panes and rested his elbows on the sill, peering out. Miko rose and joined AJ side-by-side, in the lull both had known at sea in long-ago days.

"I guess you probably have people in here babbling about god-knows-what all the time, not making any sense." The depth had returned to AJ's voice. "I scared myself two days ago. I was out of control in a way I've never felt, not even when drunk. Don't you get it? When I thought I might die one way or the other, it finally became clear to me."

"Tell me." Miko prompted calmly, sensing a precipice ahead.

"All those things people think of combat vets are true. This is just one more. It probably sounds twisted to a civilian. When your service is up, you're glad to get home. Once there, your thoughts wander back at times to that high that comes at the peak of battle, and just after. You miss it and kind of hunger for the conflict. A young man doing incredibly complex, coordinated things with a group of guys just like him—he feels his best self. You never reach that pinnacle of fear, excitement, exhilaration, adrenaline; you never see it again. That's why those four or five years remain so much a center of your life, so much of who you are. You don't realize it until you get out, that civilian life is such a letdown. And it's really hard to adjust. All this occurred to me about a year after I got home. I was going through the motions: job, etc." AJ's eyes veered sideways to Miko's. "Guys commit suicide over that let-down. You may have a long life ahead of you, and the best days of your life, in many ways, are behind you. You fear the rest of your life will be just mundane, and that you'll never be that best self again. There are lots of ways war can fuck with your head. That's just one of them. Some days, guys have to jumpstart themselves again, their thinking, that is, when they get down. You talk yourself out of that depression; or try. Just get up and go, get busy—you say to yourself, don't sit here and think about it. That's what you do—jumpstart."

The gentle rap-rap on the consult room door by an unseen staffer signaled a quarter hour past schedule. Miko spoke with mellow resolution, still at AJ's side, peering through the window with him at the familiar car lot below and the vehicles motionless there.

"I know my little game about the rooms in our minds is simple and a bit silly, when there are things that happen in our lives that make it seem like nothing is right. You have a room that holds those treasures of a time in your life that was both incredibly beautiful and incredibly ugly. But you have the strength and the brains to put it in order. You have gotten good advice from other vets, and you will have times when life lets you down, and no one seems to understand. Doctors like me may fail you; so you jumpstart yourself. That may never stop entirely. You know it's coming, and you know you can get through it. You can put that thinking on a shelf in that room of your mind, take it down and look at it, and put it back again. Never give up! The door to that room should be framed with honor. Every room belongs, every part of life has its place. If you can forgive yourself for your reactions, you may find that people want to let go of your past offenses and want to keep access to your other rooms. So much in your mental home is welcoming, AJ. Share it! Stay aware; watch your mind. Choose to honor the past but live in the happier rooms now. Be grateful to that young man you were, and that he seized experiences that most of us cannot imagine. Those maybe came too early in life, but it is what it is."

Miko sighed, searching for the right words at this passage. "I'll share this with you, AJ. My father was an uneducated fisherman—all fishermen think they are philosophers, right?" Miko scoffed. "I remember something he told me when I left for university. He said joy is not being the best at what you do; joy is getting to do the thing you are best at doing."

AJ placed his hand over his eyes, struggling to contain the tears he would heretofore have reliably stanched with anger. "You little shit Greek punk! See what you've made me do!" AJ poked, managing his trademark shit-eating grin.

Miko leaned in, eyes locked on AJ, to nail the opportunity. "But you've got to be done with mistreating your wife. That is a 'never event'—that can't be repeated, or I have an obligation to notify authorities of the risk to her. I will not hesitate. I have a duty, also. I don't share what we talk about between the two of you. But if I have any suspicion of abuse, I will take action."

"I get it, Doc. I'm still working on how to fix the damage with her. I'm not going to give you an excuse to bust me." AJ mollified.

"What about the damage to yourself, AJ? What are you going to do about your addiction to the alcohol? You know Natalia gets counseling through Al-Anon." Miko would skirt the minefield no longer. "She's doing something positive. What are you going to do? Believe me, I'm not trying to antagonize you while you're down."

"I'm not an alcoholic," AJ conveyed in a near-whisper, exhausted. "AA is for alcoholics. A craving for alcohol doesn't control me. I can drink and stop when I want. I just don't stop. That's different; it's a choice, not a craving."

"AJ, please hear me out on this. What you're saying is rational if you just think about the act of swallowing alcohol or needing to drink to avoid a painful withdrawal. Clearly, that's not your problem, yet, and may never be. Addiction, in its most simple meaning, is continued use of a substance despite harm. For whatever reason, whenever you drink to excess, that's when you do the most harm to Natalia, frighten your children, or find a gun in your hand, or . . . ," Miko paused, placing a hand on AJ's shoulder, more to steady his own passion. "Or consider taking your own life; wasting the valuable gifts you have. Can you see? Drinking isn't helping you. It's not just a social lubricant to you, and it's not responsible for your disturbing thoughts or regrets in your military or civilian life. But it is a catalyst, an on-switch to your rage. I'm not even going to talk about your physical health—you've got other risk factors for those problems, over and above the alcohol. Think, AJ, please . . ."

AJ nodded. "If it makes any difference, I'm leaving St. Frances. I turned in my notice yesterday; they asked six-month's notice to find a new chief to replace me. Nearly thirty years of being on call is enough. It's time for someone else to pick it up. I'm ready."

CHAPTER 19

NOT THERE

"It's time to decide, Miko," Sophia said slowly. Having him back in Vathi for his long-awaited visit was precious, in the home of his boyhood, where Kostas and she had played out their own timeless love story. She would shrewdly make the best of the week. The kitchen table remained ground zero for affection, joy, and laughter between mother and child once again.

Miko sat pensively, not answering the graceful dame; rather, he pondered the questions that were formulating, as he admired his mother curiously. Her aging had been graceful, still a hint of the facial beauty and svelte, upright stature that had mesmerized Kostas long ago. Her voice was softer now, and more deliberate than when Miko had returned for his father's funeral service in the middle of his Greek internship. A widow nearly two years, she nurtured the friendship of neighbors and other church-goers. Admired for her strength in solitude, not to linger upon her mourning then, people turned to her as the gentle matron entwined in their many lives. How had she done this, when closure for himself lacked an image of his father's peaceful body in a casket, and a place to visit in memorial?

"I should have been here, Momma," Miko half-whispered as he leaned toward her at the kitchen table, eyes welling. Bia was at the stove, humming and clattering dishes and pans a few feet away. Miko glanced her way, relieved that she had not overheard.

"What are you keeping from her?" Sophia whispered, leaning in toward Miko. He overtly ignored his mother's pointed observation. Sophia returned to her prior thought. "That's nonsense, my love. Don't punish yourself over nonsense. You are where you should be, and your papa was happy about your life. He didn't need to guide you, and you didn't need to protect him."

Sophia needed little verbiage to read out Miko's worries. "But I could have been with him, looking out. It's gotten to where there are few people to trust, and he was vulnerable." Miko paused, recomposing himself. "Did the police ever find anything more, any clues, or is it just closed as a random drug murder case?"

Miko knew all the evidence, having read the narrative report many times: Missing person report, filed eight days earlier. Unanchored fishing vessel registered to Kostas Papagiannis, drifting with no personnel aboard, approximately 2.5 nautical miles southeast of Salamis. Blood evidence retrieved, typed to owner, splattered on the deck and adjacent outside cabin wall; cerebral tissue and cranial bone fragments recovered in forensics. A single .44 caliber round, shallowly embedded in the upright on the rear, port cabin corner. No body recovered; no weapon discovered. Fingerprints of two other former crew who had been interrogated; alibis corroborated. Conclusion: Probable drug-related random boarding and homicide, victim's remains jettisoned; vessel abandoned in tracking phase.

"Look at me," Sophia stopping him on this path. "You see I'm doing okay. I have a happy life here in Vathi. The widow's pension is all I need, and I have lots of friends. You could not have helped your papa. You must let that thought go or it will eat at you."

"I know all this, Momma," Miko retorted sharply. "It doesn't help!" He drew a breath to calm himself. "I know. I admit this is still raw for me. I still can't bring myself to talk even with Bia about it. When I think about it, I think I'm going to lose it!"

Sophia hesitated. "As I said, it is time to decide. I've left your room all the same since you left for university. All the things from your childhood—you should go through and see what is precious to you. If America is to be your new home, take them, and leave the rest to me. On the last morning when your papa left me, he said I should go through your things soon. He knew I was missing you and feeling a bit sad, and maybe he thought it would help. What I was really feeling was sadness for your father, brave man, struggling to work and protecting me from whatever may come. I have really been in no mood to go through your things. Despite all the chaos, and his back pain, your papa had become, well, very calm. He didn't seem afraid of anything, and didn't want me to worry. He was so gentle that morning. It was his way of keeping bad things from you and me. Sometimes I wish he had not been so protective. It is strange; so strange, you know. But it worked. It is like he transferred his peacefulness to me when he was killed. And I am not afraid myself of what may come. I see the joy in each day as he did. All I need now is grandchildren! I will say no more."

"I should have been here for both of you, Momma." Miko, in turn, left it there, as Bia began loading the scrambled eggs, cheese, and tomatoes onto the table. "Anyway, I'm not in the mood, either. Going through my room will have to wait for the next time I come home."

"Okay, dear." Sophia sighed, letting Miko's dodges pass unanswered.

CHAPTER 20

WOMEN

The early Midwest freeze brought no sympathy. Fall's blazing colors had been lost on Natalia. Teaching colorful preschoolers to play and to learn through her remaining magnetism belied her other existence—cohabiting with her husband, minus intimacy. The promise of love had faded to the background of a sepia-tone portrait. Shopping was motion, not discovery; she had come to terms with the pantomime of commerce as merely a chance to hide again, alone, anonymous, safe not to regret, not to remember. The promise of her faith had proved empty, yet she prayed silently, all other power depleted. The few times she had thought about her talk with AJ's psychiatrist, she wondered why she hadn't said more or heard more. Not enough time, she rationalized—and how much would it take? Should the gentle psychoanalyst know that this coward cheated with women from work, scarcely hiding it? Would knowing change anything? She was glad, still, that he had asked about her life, and listened.

Natalia moved on to the crafts store, where purchases were still fun and fed the projects that would wire her tiny prodigies' neural pathways. There she spotted Bia, hunched over the do-it-yourself framing choices. Natalia's fast brain recalled the pleasantness of first meeting with this educated young lady, before meeting her educated young husband in clinic. Natalia trusted the calculation that Miko and Bia would not share identifiable information. It felt less than honest not to say hi again.

"Well, hello, young lady!" Natalia said crisply but softly so as to avoid startling from behind. Natalia smiled at Bia's searching reaction. "I'm Natalia. We met quite a while back in Walmart and had coffee. You were asking me about hot peppers. I wanted to ask how that went with your cooking. It's so nice to run into you again. How are you? I'm sorry, I've forgotten your name."

Bia's soft eyes and smile came together in the recollection. "Of course, Natalia, nice to see you as well. Such a surprise! I'm Bia!" she paused, recalling the encounter immediately. "Oh, yes, the peppers were quite nice—not too much and not too, too . . . just enough! Thank you. This is a pleasant surprise! We have been very well, and you?" Despite the accent and word searching, her English was more confident.

"Oh, you know, not bad; life just rolls on with the seasons. I pick up things here for my preschoolers a lot. They just love to do any little crafts and bringing them home."

"I find this store to be fun, and I was looking maybe for a picture frame, but really, just looking." Bia mused. Natalia felt good that she had approached Bia, and been so readily remembered. Bia drew a deep breath and paused. "Would you like to have coffee again? This time I buy! Do you have time?"

"I sure do! As you've probably learned, Starbucks is every-where. There's one at the end of this strip mall. Let me pay for these things real quick, and we'll go." Natalia sorted the construction paper and glue sticks in her hands, her self-isola-tion dispelled and forgotten.

Both held the warm cups in curled fingers to their faces, welcome against the chill.

"How's your husband, the doctor? If I remember correctly, I think he must still be at Public Health, right?" Natalia fished deftly for assurance of preserved confidentiality, under the circumstances.

Bia tilted her head curiously. "You remember well! Yes, Miko still has about nine months to finish in his residency."

"Well, I remembered mostly that that's why you're in Oklahoma, of all places!" Natalia laughed. "You know, Bia—that is such a lovely name—there is one question I'm curious about. Do you mind? I don't mean to get too personal."

"Of course, I will answer if I can," Bia affirmed, conveying some conditionality.

"So I've heard that in the old countries . . . ," Natalia caught herself, blushing slightly. "Ha, the old countries—it's not old to you! See, when you are born here, and you have relatives that came here from Italy or France or wherever, the old folks always seem to compare things to where they came from, and where they came from is the 'old country'—like those back home are still living in the 1940s or something. I guess all of us here have roots from somewhere else! Anyway, how did you and Miko meet? I've heard that some marriages are still arranged by parents, and the young people are just expected to go along with it. Is that right?"

"Ha-ha," Bia scoffed at the innocuous question. "Not so much now. That's pretty rare. Yes, you see some mothers and grandmothers that like to do the matchmaking—it's mostly the women—but it's not anything official; it's more like their entertainment. So, no, we were not arranged, although I know a few couples that were, and they really do quite well. I met Miko first when we were in *lykeio*, the 'high school' time here in the US. We met each other at an academic competition and dated for a while. Then I remembered him again at a party when he was in the last year at medical university, and I was in my first job in accounting. He was serious guy then, and still is, but sweet to me. For lots of reasons, he wanted to come to America for graduate training. I could see myself losing him to this goal, so I convinced him he could not live without me, and we got married just about three months before he came here for the post. He was so handsome," Bia batted her eyes, "and we just fell in love, and get along. He's very ambitious."

"So it's going well?" Natalia ran with her curiosity. Bia seemed to take the nosiness in stride. "I think I'd be scared to be just married and go to an entirely different country with a new husband."

"It's good. He's very busy. The hours are long at the hospital with patients and teaching and lectures, then he studies at home," Bia described. "We go to some dinners with his department people and a few times with my office people, but not so much. We are, you know, in a training situation for him, and we both understand it consumes our lives, and it's, well, it's okay for now."

"Bet you miss your family! I can't imagine being so far away!" Natalia was facile at drawing people out without pressure. "It must be hard for both of you!"

"Well, you might say my family is quite European, that is to say, at home anywhere on the Continent, not just Greece alone. My parents are professionals, and my two sisters' jobs have a lot of travel, so we are used to calls and emails and text, so it's not so bad." Bia's gentle smile quickly flattened. "It's funny. Miko doesn't talk about his family much. I've met his mom, of course. She came to our wedding, and we took one week of Miko's yearly holiday to visit her, umm, four or five months ago. She's very pleasant, and I like her, but we don't visit often. I think Miko feels bad that he does not see her more. So it's like there is a part of him that I don't know, and he doesn't share much of it with me or anyone else." Bia caught herself momentarily, then lowered her voice. "His father was a fisherman and lost at sea. There was some crime suspected, but nothing was ever solved."

"Oh, my god, Bia," Natalia gasped, eyes and mouth wide. "That's awful!"

"Yes. Miko does not talk about it with me. Miko is the one child of his parents. His grandfather lived with them when he was small child, and Miko doesn't remember much about him. So not a big family. It seems to bring him sadness. He says there is little to tell about. Sometimes, he talks about his father's fishing boat, and how he enjoyed that when he was small. And that week with his mother, you know, it didn't help me to learn more. Ha! We were jet-lagged all the time there and jet-lagged when we came back to here! Oh, but now, a coincidence, soon, Miko will take his second week leave and go home to see his mother by himself. I haven't stored up enough time at my job to go again. It's okay. It's like much of the time he is away when he's here."

"Well, I'm sure it will be wonderful for his mother. She's probably so proud to have her son be successful as a doctor, right?" Natalia asked.

"Yes, yes, they are still quite close. He calls her most weeks." Bia scoffed, rolling her eyes. "With his busy schedule, sometimes I think he talks to his mother more than he talks to me!"

Natalia took notice as Bia's gaze wandered beyond the café windows and back to her cup. "That sounds familiar." Natalia commiserated. "You know, sometimes people, especially men, get so wrapped up in their work, it's like they live two separate lives. Not that they mean to do it, but, I think, they just don't see themselves doing it. Huh, I think that's why a lot of people, again, mostly men, have affairs. They get disconnected from what was important to them at one time."

Bia's gaze shot to Natalia's face and as quickly broke off, her eyes sweeping about the table. The women sat quietly for a moment amid the din of the barista's commerce. Natalia puzzled as Bia's face became flush. Setting her coffee down, Bia gathered her jacket and handbag.

"I should be going, now." Bia announced.

"Are you okay?" Natalia asked.

"Yes, of course. I just remembered some things I need to finish. Sorry. I should go now. Thank you, Natalia, for such a pleasant time," Bia smiled and grasped Natalia's forearm, as women did in her upbringing.

Natalia reaching for a pen and notepad in her handbag. "I'm giving you my number. I think we should get together and just spend a day shopping and have lunch, maybe on one of the preschool breaks, you know?" Would you like that? You let me know. Okay?" Natalia said with kind finality, passing the note.

Bia nodded, folding the paper without inspection, and slipped it into a blouse front pocket. "Maybe when Miko goes to his mother again in the next month or two, I will call you! And we will not talk about your husband's treatment by my husband; that would be breaking the rules, and I don't want to get Miko in trouble. On the other hand, it's maybe a little exciting to be almost breaking the rules!"

CHAPTER 21
INTUITION

In the beginning of their sojourn in the US, Bia considered the transition a part of the natural cycle of training life, so it was not really a topic of discussion on the occasions the two socialized among the staff at faculty functions. Maybe because she was a trailing spouse with no other specific reason to be in middle-America, the lack of distraction made the cultural shift feel more defined to her. Miko's growing confidence turned a corner when, for the first time, he became senior to the younger trainees. He dressed and groomed with added authority; punctuality became purposeful rather than reactive. His clinic schedule was full and controlled, with as much onus on mentoring the junior residents as his own learning. The seriousness came with less small talk about her days and the larger world, less laughter and intimacy. He would often deflect her probing, asserting to be working through recent new cases in his head.

When he did confide in her, mostly before rolling over to sleep, he shared with her how, thanks to the new flag system designating the sequence of exam offices to be entered, he could unabashedly saunter through the institution's corridors looking straight ahead and avoiding eye contact with patients seated along the walls. Amid the suffering captured within those buildings, he had explained, the so-called 'interesting patient' was nothing but a myth—a protective euphemism for those who could not to turn away from the burden of that suffering. 'Physician, heal thyself'—another tortured cliché—would whisper in his moments of self-assessment, he had told her. Miko was one of the specialty residents who could arrange time to teach in the Master of Social Work and Physician Assistant programs. The meager extra earnings went to savings the two would need when repatriating to Greece at the end of his training. His own level of debt from medical school was non-existent in comparison to that of several of the US-graduate residents, often exceeding a quarter of a million dollars. He complained to Bia of witnessing the corrosion, that the debt was instrumental in transforming the dreamy-eyed humanists he was training with into drowning and mercenary drones targeted on future potential earnings. His professional growth belied an amorphous anxiety. In addition to the weight of these worries, Bia wondered what she was missing from Miko's conversations with his mother.

Even on overcast days, the morning light flowed more optimistically into Bia's cubicle on the fourth floor of the PSO building than into most other forgotten downtown Tulsa structures. Few co-workers had noticed she'd been given this choice corner view of the hospital across the tops of the patch-work of aged edifices from the past half-century.

From her perch, Bia had occasionally caught a glimpse of Miko scurrying to and from the education annex appended to the sick house, as the in-patient building was unaffectionately referred to among trainees. Just those flashes of connection in the middle of the day tantalized her. Even married now nearly three years, she remained in the volcanic phase of their relationship and still ogled at his masculine lines and confident stride, wavy hair tousling in the wind as he plowed his course through what may come.

Leaving the building, he often walked slower, talking and gesturing with one or more students, even stopping as if patiently answering questions from his tiny, engaged entourage. On these occasional distant sightings, one figure would be seen more frequently on the Tuesday-Thursday routine. Unlike the shapeless scrub apparel of the other disciples, a svelte, auburn figure was consistently layered elegantly with impeccably seasonal colors, and able to negotiate an icy pavement casually in calf-high boots. On some colder days with wind in their faces, she had been Miko's sole accompaniment. On a day of ice-glazed sidewalks, they navigated arm-in-arm until their respective destinies diverged at the passage's bifurcation. Today, the pair would pause, holding two hands together; a moment's chat, then she gave him three kisses on alternating cheeks, and as quickly, each set off without looking back.

The PSO building was conveniently situated in a virtual straight shot, five blocks walk from the dungeon. By now, she could make it to or from in nine minutes, blindfolded. She had not gathered many names along the way, yet a series of amiable porch-sitters and shopkeepers had emerged over time who would wave to her and smile their welcome on each quiet passing. Her bashfulness with English restrained her approaching them even now. Nonetheless, Bia had created a familiar village unto herself and needed little more. So American, yet now familiar, even the Starbucks, barely notable around the gently curved lane going north, did not disturb the ambiance of the imaginary kibbutzim she had created for her own psycho-emotional sustainability; until it did.

Bia did not miss anything that changed along her daily route, least of all the pre-spring seed offerings displayed in the crates outside the diminutive Middle Eastern store. She imagined a close, second-generation family would inhabit the living space over the shop, hawking both kosher and halal, across from the comparably cosmopolitan coffee culture-piece run by immigrant cousins. Obscured in the evening's light shower, she glimpsed an attractive couple at a window-side table, faces turned from the steamy glass as if to avoid observation from outside. Bia strained for plausible deniability, despite the familiar shapes and Miko's characteristic slouch and habit of running one hand straight back through his fluffy hair. A thousand competing thoughts flooded her mind as hot blood rushed to her face. Rising to the top was how he could be so obvious, this close to the dungeon, in a town with so many other tryst opportunities? She gasped a breath, oblivious of the time passed since she had drawn the one before. Her whole middle felt tight. A wave of nausea brought her near to one knee momentarily, while a rush of saliva filled her mouth. Had the whole calculus of their existence together just shifted?

She would not look back and cursorily touched the undulating vertical surfaces of the row of shops to keep her balance as she hurried along, breaking from the support only to cross the street and finish the direct path to the dungeon house. Every few moments, she would close her eyes and tilt her chin up to catch the cooling rain on her cheeks and forehead.

She would not ask. She would not react in front of him. She would look for the right moment to probe. It was too soon, and she was not ready to hear whatever he would have to say. She was Bia. Bia had self-control. Bia was not the stereotypical raging Mediterranean woman. She was Bia, who had never felt so needy nor so alone. She thought of Natalia, her shopping acquaintance, and how long Natalia had been married, wondering what it takes to get to a place like that. She again mulled calling Natalia when Miko goes to see his mother.

CHAPTER 22

SCUTTLEBUTT

The chill had returned to the clinic building. AJ filled the few minutes' wait for Miko pondering how, if he were in charge of power here, he'd find a way to work with HVAC to stabilize the too warm / too chilly bipolar climate in the old clinic building, or just raze the damn thing and start over. He'd keep his advice to himself as Miko rounded the heavy door. AJ remembered when he was young and could maintain the breathless pace that Miko kept up between their now bimonthly conversations. Not anymore, he thought. This young man was growing confident before his eyes over the time of their encounters. The dynamic of patient-hood had softened into conversations.

"So what's your day been like so far, Doc? Done any exorcisms this morning?" AJ mused.

"No, no, AJ, we leave that to the clergy affiliated with social services." Miko fired back and chuckled. "Seriously, though, while we should not compare patients, you should consider the good things you have. For example, you can actually think and hold an agreed reality and some insights in your head. You may not be surprised to know that a guy in my profession spends a lot of time each day simply adjusting medicines to help many people just keep their feet on the ground, so to speak, and not hallucinate or hear voices telling them to do bad things. I must say, I like this part of the job better, the clinical psychology, having good conversations with guys like you."

"Yeah, I guess guys like me are a whole other circus of clowns! But I'd guess you also hear some interesting stuff from us. And most of the scary or bizarre shit really happened!" AJ countered.

"Exactly, AJ." Miko affirmed. He paused, ostensibly reviewing the records on the monitor screen. "It doesn't seem possible, but I haven't seen you in four months, and it looks like you canceled an appointment in July, let's see; and then you rescheduled for now. Sorry, I know my schedule has been pretty packed in the last several months. I appreciate your patience. It's good to see you again. Let me ask you to fill me in, before we get started on what I'd like to follow up on."

"Happy to," AJ responded cheerfully. "Last time I was in, actually—maybe you remember—it was on an unscheduled visit when I, well, sort of went off the deep end."

"I recall, AJ." Miko affirmed.

"You pointed out the connection between alcohol and my, let's say, lapses in disposition."

"Nicely put, AJ. I recall that as well."

"I canceled the appointment after that. You made your point well. I didn't go to AA or anything like that. I took a couple of weeks and stayed at a private facility near Tahlequah that caters confidentially to executives, clergy, and some vets—an odd combination of clientele—that's run by what they call addictionologists. Another vet pointed me there. It was a good experience. First they monitor you for some days to make sure you don't get the shakes and other serious crap during withdrawal while they make sure you're avoiding any booze. Then, mostly, they get you on a healthy diet, get you back to a reasonable exercise program, and on to what they call behavioral modification, where you learn to think about alternatives to anger, or whatever leads you to drink. That's about it." AJ summarized.

"And how's it going with what you learned, AJ?"

"Well, I wanted to thank you for kicking my ass to do something. I'm getting to be a codger, but I've learned I don't know everything, and I need to listen. I learned a lot there—many good ideas that I can take on. Natalia's always tried to feed me a good heart diet; she's glad that I'm becoming more plant-based. I take that as a good sign that she wants me to live—ha, ha." AJ scoffed sarcastically. "I'm seeing how much anger I've carried, anger about insignificant things about people and the choices they make, or how they are. I'm still learning to watch that bullshit rise up in me. The world's been black and white to me; like people are either wrong or right. I'm seeing more that there's a range between points on the meter. And people are who they are, each of us has our own strengths and weaknesses. At least, I'm thinking about it. Can't say that I'm enlightened yet. The addictionologist was more blunt than you, Doc. Says it takes longer to get to 'like ourselves' than it does to get sober. I've got a way to go before I'm Mr. Nice Guy. I can't bullshit Natalia. It's going to be a challenge to rebuild what I've busted over and over with her. But, hey, I'm up for the challenge as long as she doesn't throw me out! Yeah, maybe I did peak too early, but you can't have wars just so jokers like me can get their thrills. The battles I've been fighting since have been of my own making."

Miko gazed at his desk pad, feigning notetaking with a swirling doodle, and pursed his lips to avoid exuding a giddy grin with AJ's hint of progress. "I'm glad to hear about the insights you've gained, AJ. Keep at it. You can learn new tricks.

There are no guarantees for any of us. Don't count the skirmishes; look for the long wins."

AJ nodded.

"Do you realize that we've been on this path together nearly a year and a half?" Miko recounted. "It may be getting close to the time when you will want to fire me, so I'll stop badgering you."

"Maybe so," AJ grinned. "Guess you've taught me all you know, and I still don't know nothin'!"

"Before you do, I think we both need to ask again about the night long ago when the police brought you into the ER, drunk and disorderly, with a weapon—one bullet in the mechanism. Let's revisit that event, may we? It still is not clear to me, and possibly not to you, what was on your mind at that time. We're you considering harming yourself or someone else, in going out in public armed? Let's revisit the thoughts of that night, if you can remember. Take your time."

AJ stroked his chin slowly a few times and drew himself up in the armchair. "Yeah, okay. I knew we'd eventually get here. I don't know how you make your notes, but I'll try to address it. I should." AJ exhaled heavily and began.

"My sister's husband got under my skin a long time ago. Karli, if I hadn't told you before, was the oldest of us six kids, about four years older than me. Long story short, she's got a heart of gold, but the brains of a rabbit. She spent part of high school in a convent and was very religious. But then she left the convent, and a year or so out of high school, she and a friend got a bug up their butts to get out of Tulsa, so they joined the goddamned Marine Corps. About a year into her tour, she got pregnant, got an honorable discharge, got married, and moved to New York. She lived there for a few years with or around her husband Joe's family. Eventually, they had three boys, and things seemed to be going reasonably well. Joe's family—his name is Joe Daconta—seemed to treat Karli well, and for an Okie girl, she seemed to adapt to New York okay.

"Who knew why they left Brooklyn to move to Tulsa, but I suspect Joe was dodging some shit even back then. He's a liar, and lazy as hell. What's worse is he knows it and is proud of it. Karli's only fault was she couldn't see through his bullshit for so long, and when she finally did, she stayed with the shithead for a long list of excuses—the kids, her vows, yadda-yadda. She took a vow when she entered the convent when she was fifteen and was able to walk away from that! So why wasn't she able to walk away from the bastard who knocked her up when she was a naive marine recruit? Becoming this city cop in Tulsa was the perfect set up for him to pull off the same shit his daddy did as a Brooklyn cop. Joe relished that kind of life.

"'You know, Jamie,' Joe would bullshit, 'I've got a degree from City College of New York. I hung out there with the Jewish kids, because they were the smart ones. What you learn is to let the other dumb bastards bust their asses, and you take the gravy. You know why? 'Cause the others are suckers who follow the rules and think it matters.' Joe would sit back in a leather recliner in his den, filled with some of the nicest furniture I'd ever touched, surrounded by his elaborate gun displays and Marine emblems and paraphernalia. "I didn't want to be a marine," Joe would say, "I wanted to be an ex-marine. Everybody thinks you're some kind of hardened hero if you're an ex-marine. It's immediate respect! During my tour, I spent my two years active as a lifeguard at the officers' club. I almost never wore the uniform. At official functions, all the officers would be in alpha uniforms or even mess dress, and I'd be tooling around in swim trunks and a tank top! Yeah, I spent three months in Vietnam when we were training them to hold an old US M-1 rifle. I was still a lifeguard at the officers' club there! This was all before the war broke out. I got the service ribbon anyway. It's in the frame over there on the wall with the other stuff.'

"I thought it was just sort of the New York nonsense. Karli was happy . . . or seemed so. We first thought Joe was being good to her in coming to Tulsa, her hometown. I think he just saw a mark in this town, and that her family would carry them until his real ambitions played out. As time went on, most of my suspicions were validated.'

Ψ

"'So you're Daconta's brothers-in-law?' asked Jimmy Jones, the off-duty TPD officer. Mike and I would have a few laughs with Jimmy at Arnie's, an obscure, but cozy neighborhood bar just east of downtown. Jimmy was a joker and a bit puffed-up himself with his flashy rings and sunglasses, even keeping the shades on inside at the dimmer end of Arnie's long, dark, classic wooden bar. He had done two years in the Guard and seen some riot action. He seemed to hold combat veterans with an extra measure of respect, and because he did, the respect was returned to him, even if he was a bit of a showboat. 'I'm surprised!'

"'You know Joe?' Mike asked the obvious, politely.

"'Everyone on the force knows Joe Daconta.' Jimmy waded in, watching our facial reactions to see if this was okay territory or not. 'He's the current President of the Fraternal Order of Police branch here, you know, the FOP. I don't want to cast aspersions. So he's married to your sister?'

"'Yeah, bub.' I replied. 'He's kind of a dickhead, but, yeah, that's him. Karli's blind. She thinks he's great. She stays mad at me that I won't give him the time of day. I don't trust him.' I paused. 'Why? You know something we don't?' I didn't think I was betraying any news to anyone who really knew Joe.

"Jimmy liked to look at himself in a mirror, not unlike a few cops I know, but we took him for being honest, and a rule follower. Jimmy then said, 'Most guys on the force don't really care for Joe Daconta, either. He's suspected of shaking down some small businesses, especially on the north side, you know, the colored night clubs and so forth. If something goes down, and he's your nearest back-up, people don't count on him to show anymore—like he's not going to risk it. It's not out in the public domain yet, but he's being investigated for bringing an automatic rifle to a bust for open gambling at a black joint where he was taking protection money. He shot up the joint and scared the shit out of a bunch of people, while laughing his ass off, enjoying watching all these dressed-up colored people running for the door, slipping and sliding. The rookie that was with him that night has quit, and they can't find him to file a report or make a statement. When some prominent black folk filed a complaint, Daconta called in a debt on someone with the local NAACP, who is now about to vouch for his character and propriety. He gets away with all kinds of shit like that.'

"'I'm not surprised.' Mike chimed in quietly. 'Karli's a bit dumb and sees what she wants to see. She brags about the police all the time and thinks Joe's a saint. Maybe she gets that from comparing Joe to me and AJ,' Mike laughed. 'You see, Joe likes to bash us for our faults in front of the rest of the family, so maybe there's some fodder there. But he's a chicken shit—he won't say anything to our faces.'

"'Well, maybe I've said enough.' Jimmy mused, smiling at the bubbles in his beer. 'I'm sure your sister's a very nice person, but I'll tell you guys, Daconta is known as the biggest womanizer on the force. It's blatant. No one knows how he gets away with it. So I guess she is blind. Wouldn't want to be you telling her. But that's up to you.'

Jimmy and Mike watched me, sitting silently, staring at my beer mug and spinning around a pack of matches on the table.

Ψ

"Mike was sweet." AJ went on. "You remember Mike and Greg are my two younger, twin brothers. They were both good sailors, but kind of misfits in the Navy, always in trouble for something, usually getting back late from shore leave for one lame reason or another. I loved them both. Mike and I got really close after Greg's suicide. I guess we needed each other.

"As for Joe, I wondered where all this was leading. At that moment, I don't think I had the heart to burst my sister's bubble. I had an aching feeling that, someday, someone was going to have to set Joe straight. I hoped to god it would be someone else, before me. I know how I get to be sometimes, when I've been drinking. It's like all the chains have been pulled off, and I feel like I've got to do something that needs doing. It's usually saying something that needs to be said or setting some asshole straight by whooping his ass. It's kind of a compulsion to do what one's got to do. And the next day, I'm usually not sure what it was all about."

"AJ," Miko's tone carried some urgency, face flushed in embarrassment. "Before we go on about this situation with Joe and your sister, I want you to tell me more about your brother Greg. You mentioned his suicide, something I'm unaware of. I just glanced back at the Family History section in your record, and there's no mention of suicide in your immediate family members. So Greg was Mike's twin, right? Can you tell me more about his death? When it happened, under what circumstances, and how it affected you?"

"Yeah, well, I didn't mean to let that slip. It's not something we talk about. I think we have all talked about it enough and have moved on. By we, I mean the family." AJ shifted in his seat uncomfortably, scratching his head.

"I won't make you talk about this, AJ, if you are not ready and willing to," Miko led further. "You seem to have been close to all your brothers, perhaps the twins especially, since they were closer to your age. Mike and you became closer, you said, when you both lost Greg. I'm curious about the nature of Greg's illness when he ended his life."

"I don't know about any illness," AJ cleared his throat. "Yeah, I knew he got depressed sometimes, but he didn't go on about it. It was like he'd get the blues, like anyone else." AJ paused, staring nowhere. "Greg had a need to be important, you know, he wanted to be somebody. That was when you could get into chiropractic school after two years of college. I do believe he was probably excellent with his hands; people have told me that. Most of all, I think he wanted to be called 'doctor.' But along the way there, he spent like a big shot on cars and houses and got deep in debt and got sideways with his wife and kids. Had problems with a couple of business part-ners. He and his wife separated, and like an idiot, he left their home in Green Bay and moved back to Oklahoma alone. I think he was coming apart then and just wanted to be around Mike and the rest of the family. He could only afford to bring his three kids down for a visit once a year and eventually had to borrow more money just to do that. When his wife wanted to get remarried, I think that put him over the edge—the thought of someone else being like a father to his kids."

"That sounds like quite a spiral." Miko affirmed.

"You know, the night before the funeral, we were all together, I mean, the five of us kids. And things just let loose. Karli said that Joe once told Greg that if Joe himself had Greg's problems, he'd probably shoot himself, and so Joe was worried he may have planted the idea. Yeah, I'll bet he was worried! Karli was angry at Greg, saying, 'How could he be so selfish and do this to us.' Mike described in vivid detail how Greg came over just to have company and maybe work on his tan in the backyard. While Mike was making sandwiches, he heard the shotgun blast. Apparently, as soon as Mike had left the living room, Greg quickly got Mike's shotgun, loaded it, walked out to the yard, and blew his head off, in a manner of speaking. Mike wasn't saying much, but he told us all how he'd found Greg—even what Greg looked like when he found him, but in a way that we all could take—to give us some sort of closure, since it would be a closed-casket funeral. It was just Mike again, being the kind one, in a way his sister and brothers understood. For the rest, maybe he was just letting us say out loud what he was thinking and feeling, without arguing."

Miko held the silence, watching the bewilderment arrive and dissolve over AJ's composure.

"I miss him. I guess it is hard to talk about, so I avoid it." AJ rationalized. "I wish I could have been able to give him some money, but he didn't ask me—probably thinking I couldn't afford it. I wish I could have been closer and watched him better. Yeah, we were all adults, but I'm still his big brother, goddammit! I was mad at Joe and Karli and Greg's wife and everybody else, but madder at myself." Clearing his throat and nasal passages, AJ managed in a terse whisper, "I let him down. I can't undo that. It's unbelievable that he's gone, and I'm still here. At least he had the courage to be decisive—I think there's some honor in that. Better than me."

"May I say something, AJ?" Miko entered softly.

"Absolutely, Doc. That's why I'm still here in your office, so you can weigh in on shit like this."

Miko rounded the desk gently without fully rising, taking a skewed seat on the desk's front edge, and pressed a measured touch momentarily on his patient's forearm. "I'm so sorry for your loss of your dear brother Greg. I hope that time will bring you some measure of comfort. As a doctor, I won't quote you any unhelpful statistics about depression and its fatal outcome, but there's a few things I'd like you to consider when thinking about Greg. Probably everyone around you has recommended that you remember Greg in the good times, and I certainly endorse that. But let me tell you some things about the disorder that led to his death, without the stigma or the shame that people often associate with taking one's own life."

AJ nodded, drawing a deep sigh.

"It's true that a person may take their own life for some higher purpose, like sparing someone else, perhaps family or loved ones, from being affected in an impossible situation. That's the rare occurrence. Most self-annihilation occurs as the natural history of depression. The 'natural history' of any fatal disease is the course it takes if not interrupted by treatment. Depression, at its long-bearing worst, is one of most physically painful things that humans attempt to bear—and I mean physically. It's an ache in the middle of your gut that, as it grows, takes your breath away, like someone wrapping thick tape round and round your chest until you can barely speak. The factors in each person's life that drive him or her into that depth of despair are too many to talk about, and different for everyone. The pain builds while we struggle to find fixes for our lives, only to lose control of our thinking, and watch the image of ourselves cruelly melt into worthlessness. When the person cannot stand the pain any longer, a solution magically presents itself, out of thin air, something he or she may have fantasized about in passing—a window, a bridge, a gun, or something to swallow and put themselves into the restful sleep they haven't had for so long—and they can no longer think straight. The solution draws them into its vortex, pulling them ever more strongly, until at some moment, they run full force toward it to get away from the pain that is already strangling them. In that moment, it appears to be the most rational decision we will ever make."

AJ's eyes followed hypnotically as Miko, letting the lesson marinate, rounded the desk back to his swivel chair, where he resumed an authoritative posture—elbows on chair arms, hands prayerfully over chest.

"The survivors—the loved ones who remain—almost invariably look for an external reason, something or someone with causality. In the end, suicide is the most personal act one will ever take. The depressed person no longer has room to consider others or what others are thinking—they simply want the pain to stop. It is entirely natural for loved ones to dwell and blame—those are elements of the sadness in deep and unexpected loss. Yet blame is entirely unrelated to the fallen one. Imagine if a hidden infection or a cancer had swallowed your brother. At some point in the disease progression, there was no saving him. My specialty works every day to get there in time and turn the forces around. Given a chance, we often do well. Sometimes we lose, no matter what we do, just like in other medical illnesses—illnesses also not caused by any friend or loved one. Loved ones have no power or influence over those other causes of death. Yet survivors imagine they could have for someone who dies by their own hand. Depression is another physical battle that some humans in the world are going to face and may not survive. Nobody gets the credit nor the blame. We may pledge to do better the next time, if we get the chance. Some people in our society even scoff at suicidal gestures, acts that are not likely to kill anyone, pursued as a cry for help, as if the person in pain doesn't have the guts to do it. Believe me, those are the times when we in healthcare get a break; we get a reasonable chance to intervene before the vortex takes over. So miss your brother Greg who passed naturally and keep your love of him in your heart. And keep telling stories about him and your lives together, before he became ill and died."

AJ mumbled a muffled acknowledgment, nodding his acceptance of the comfort in Miko's revelations with an innocent awkwardness. "You called it a 'vortex.' I may have gotten a taste of that in the vault at St. Francis. If Greg was at that point, now I get it."

"Let's stop here for today." Miko suggested. "We were getting at your tensions with your brother-in-law, and learning about Greg was a detour. I'm glad we had the chance to talk about your brother. We'll set up another regular interval appointment for you, but, if you can be flexible, I'm going to find an opening for us to get back within the next couple of weeks, so we can continue to understand your state of mind when you first came to us. I think we need some closure on that incident."

CHAPTER 23

fOP LEADEP

Arolling sea counts cadence at the shoreline; men count the seasons of their lives with similar significance. Amid the time demands in the clinic and wards, study and lectures on the advancing pharmacology in his field, and the pajama time spent catching up on documentation, Miko saved the daily walks to and from the medical center for his psychological time. In this realm of mindlessness, however brief, he practiced recharging his purposefulness and expelling the noise. More often now, he would sense the gentle essence of his papa with him, uttering some vague wisdom.

Arranging a position for his return to Greece could no longer wait. The coming visit with his mother in Vathi in early December, before beginning his final six months of residency, would coincide with Miko's scheduled job interviews. AJ Connolly's name on the Monday schedule again so soon bode well in hope of another goal line crossed before Miko would finish his training program.

"This morning, AJ, as you will remember, I would like to see us connect the dots on what you're telling me about your brother-in-law Joe and the events of the night you came with

"

the police to our emergency department many months back. Let's see if we can get there. Are you still okay with that?"

"Sure, Doc. I'll wind it up here pretty quickly. I know I keep saying that." AJ clasped his hands and stared distantly as he approached the matter. "You know, being on call for 24/7/365 wears you down, with little energy for anything else. Maybe I was a little jealous. See, I was one of those working stiffs Joe would criticize for being stupid, and taking responsibility, and being on call until I was bone-tired. And there he was, looking fresh and rested, clean, and clearly bringing in way more money than any cop I'd met, and tons more than I was bringing in by busting my ass. So Joe's so-called retirement almost put me over the edge.

"Maybe that's why Joe got to me. Eventually, I couldn't stand to be in the same room with him, let alone to talk with him. At family get-togethers, if he showed up, I'd just leave. I knew if I started in, it would get ugly. He was my sister's husband, and everyone else seemed to like him, and he was a policeman as well.

"Joe was big. About 240 lbs., six-foot two, big hands. Always clean-shaven like a bank executive, and neat haircut, slicked back. He was all New York. You'd never see him in work clothes or blue jeans in all the years he was in Oklahoma. Always acted smarter and better than everyone else in the room.

"One Saturday afternoon, Jimmy had pulled by the house in his squad car and he saw me out working in the front yard.

"'Hey, dumb ass! How's things at the big house?' Jimmy chided. More than once, Jimmy had mused about how St. Francis had grown bigger than the penitentiary in McAllister, and how it had had a hold on me for so long. I had always countered that Jimmy was the one person who could preen around like a peacock without me wanting to take him down a peg or two. I had seen Jimmy drop all pretense and take charge more than once at Arnie's, when a brawl might break out. Arnie always appreciated that.

"'I've been working in the yard all day. Don't make me have to whip your ass out here in front of the neighbors.' I was glad to see Jimmy.

"'Yeah, yeah, you worthless piece of Navy shit. You think I drove out of my way to watch you sweat? Listen, just wanted to give you a heads up. It's about Joe Daconta. Thought you should hear it from me. But keep it to yourself.' Jimmy paused. 'There's a lot of pissed-off cops in Tulsa. I don't want your sister to get into the fray somehow, if something gets sparked.'

"'Alright, drama queen. Nothing would surprise me. What now?' I was kneeling, listening while I wiped the gritty oil and grass off the lawn mower.

"'Well, your dearly beloved brother-in-law is a bully. You probably know that. He brags to the city council like he's the world's model of policing, since as the president of the FOP, he's never discharged his service revolver in the line of duty. Well, there's a half dozen or more patrol officers who refuse to ride with him, because the big son-of-a-bitch is wicked with a blackjack or nightstick. He's had a number of complaints for excessive force—especially on anyone with dark skin or long hair. So far, other guys have given in to backing him up, saying the perps were resisting arrest, and so forth. The women officers would never ride with him in the first place.'

"'Why are you telling me this, Jimmy? Don't you have Internal Affairs or something to deal with that.' My thoughts unfortunately went immediately to my brother Mike, and the time, in a drunken rage over nothing, I took a tire iron to Mike's jaw, resulting in the need for extensive dental work. There was a pang of guilt, lest I be too critical of Joe's brutality.

"'It's beyond that. Joe was found to have embezzled a huge amount of cash from the FOP funds over the past ten years. Internal Affairs has nailed him for it, but not before he took a nightstick to the desk officer who stupidly confronted him before going to the chief. Well, no one has proved it was Joe who beat the guy up. The poor son-of-a-bitch desk guy is at your big house now and may not ever speak again. What Joe didn't know was that the desk cop had already spoken to an auditor, so it has all unraveled. So get this, the chief and Public Affairs have made a deal with Joe. He agrees to resign without any press on this to save face for the city. Now, there's rumbling that if Joe stays in town, some alternative justice is in the brew. You didn't hear this from me. Much of it is just scuttlebutt now.'

"'Son of a bitch,' I told Jimmy. 'Now it all makes sense. Joe and Karli have a 'for sale' sign in front of their house and have already moved to one of those month-to-month apartments before the house has even sold. She says they want to move to Florida for their retirement to be near Joe's aging parents. She probably knows nothing of this FOP business. Hearing from me about Joe's dirty business will just seem like trash talk to her. But you can tell your brothers-in-arms that the Dacontas are leaving the state, if that does any good.'

CHAPTER 24

THE MARK

"When it rains, it pours." AJ's rush of speech picked up as he recounted his mounting disgust. "Not two days after Jimmy's stop-by, I got a call from the old man, you know, my dad. Said he'd been talking to Karli over a period of time about Momma's sister Dona. Dona was a widow, and her husband Uncle Johnny had been a trucker with his own rig and made pretty good money at that before he died, as well as from the proceeds from two grasshopper oil jack-pumps on his land near Sapulpa. Uncle Johnny had accumulated quite a bit of cash from those. Like Mom, Dona had Alzheimer's and was living in a nursing home by then. Dona and Johnny had no kids, so when Dona dies, Mom and her kids would be their heirs. Dad met me at the door when I drove to his place in the countryside. He looked worried.

"Dad said he, as Mom's next of kin, agreed with Dona's banker that under the circumstances, Joe and Karli could become Dona's guardians and power of attorney. Dad couldn't do it, looking after our mother and all, and figured none of the other kids could do it working full time. Now that Joe and

Karli are both retired, and Karli wanted to do it, it seemed like the best option.

"I agreed with the old man that it sounded like a reasonable arrangement. Karli's been better than the rest of us at keeping track of everybody.

"Dad went on that he had just got a call from the banker yesterday to inform Dad that he had notified the Tulsa County Sheriff's office of suspected bank fraud. Their division had tracked the movement of Dona's money through a series of banks, the latest being that the funds had been split into two wires to Florida banks. Dad didn't know what to do, but thought us boys were being screwed. He felt that he could take care of Mom, and didn't need the money. He was given the name of someone in the district attorney's office who we could call about the investigation.

"I sat on one of the plastic chairs just outside Dad's back porch in the shade of the elm tree overhanging the pond where I used to fish with my brothers. This was all land that Aunt Dona and Uncle Johnny had owned at one time and had given Dad a good price on for a section. It was a humid day, and Dad brought out glasses of ice tea.

"I told him, 'Dad, I know you feel bad now, but I'm kind of relieved that you see what I've seen in Joe all these years. You always want to see the best in someone.' I rolled that cold tea glass across my forehead wishing it was something stronger. 'But, the truth is, you and Mom could use any money left when Dona goes, way more than Joe and Karli, or any of the rest of us kids. Even I didn't think Joe was capable of screwing his own family. I don't know what we can do, but maybe I'll call that attorney fella on Monday and ask. I'll make this right somehow. And Joe will pay, sooner or later, one way or another.'"

Miko redirected. "Before we wind up, AJ, what was your frame of mind then? It sounds like this matter was for the police. So how did the situation get to you having a loaded pistol and found drunk on the streets by the police? And is your stress with your brother-in-law still ongoing? Didn't it make sense to you just to call that district attorney in the first place?"

AJ gazed down to the drab linoleum floor a moment before raising dead eyes, peering at Miko from a head cocked low, jaw muscles grinding menacingly. Silenced by the metamorphosis, Miko sat puzzled.

"Who the fuck are you to tell me what makes sense, piss-ant? Hell, you've been a professional student your whole life, never a worry, talking all the time like some know-it-all about shit you know nothing about. Well, fuck you and the horse you rode in on! What makes sense to me with someone like Joe is that someone needs to take that motherfucker down a notch or two in a way he will never forget, and maybe he won't be the pretty boy any longer. A simple tire iron can speak volumes. You might see a little sense it that, asshole. Do you think?"

Miko's right hand went reflexively to his desk's front edge that hid the panic button meant to be deployed swiftly when physical confrontation in a clinic space seemed eminent. He paused before pressing. Heat rose in his face, pulse hastening, like a five-year-old child barked at cruelly by an ill-tempered grandfather. Witnessing setbacks is scarier than reading about them, Miko reckoned. The chill passed quickly; composure held intact.

"AJ, I'm sorry. I can see you are upset. You're right. I asked the question in a judgmental way, and I did not mean to. Getting angry with me is understandable and I accept it. Unfortunately, it won't help us; it won't help you. This is clearly a very sensitive issue for you. We need to unpack it and better understand it." Miko paused, noting the de-escalating redness in AJ's face.

"Correct me if I'm wrong." Miko reasoned. "You get entirely incensed at people picking on others who are weaker, just like with your little brothers, and you want to tear into them yourself, rather than go to some school principal or the police. Let me know if that is anywhere near what you are feeling right now. Maybe your urge to fight and your protective instincts are two sides of the same coin."

The old clock's ticking filled the void. AJ's gaze fell back to the floor, hands releasing their grip on the chair that Miko envisioned as a potential projectile.

"You're probably not far off." AJ mustered in a shrunken voice, frozen in the sober daylight by the specter of his own outsized and misplaced volatility.

"I may be a piss-ant, whatever that is, AJ, but I will not tell you what to feel. I know you want results that matter and to not get into more trouble. No one responds favorably to anger, and name-calling, because nobody is listening when you go there." Miko searched AJ's face for feedback. "I know I'm pushing, but I want to hear what we've been avoiding— tell me what happened the night when you were brought to the hospital. We need to go there."

AJ folded his arms across his chest and exhaled heavily. "You want an answer," he began, eyes searching the floor. "I guess we both need an answer." AJ rubbed his chin, forehead and temples, and reached around with his right hand to scratch his lower back, mannerisms Miko had come to link with AJ's organizing his thoughts. "I knew Jimmy meant well to let me know that Karli risked collateral damage if a group of patrol officers, each having a beef with Joe, targeted him. I had worked in the yard and frankly, intended to sneak off and enjoy a cold one or two, and think things over. There's another hole-in the-wall place called Gracie's between home and St. Francis that's good for that, especially if you want to be alone. A gnawing in my gut that had set in after Jimmy's drop-by gradually grew into something that needed to be expelled. Small irritating factors sometimes seem to concentrate into one big deal, almost like that vortex thing you talked about before. Something needed to be done about Joe; it just seemed like a responsibility I was avoiding. The only detail around the margins that lingered was the given that I would go to jail for a long time. The rest of my life would be wrecked or gone. And pissed at her or not, if Karli got hurt in a police hit, it would be my failure and I wasn't sure if I would be able to live that down.

"Gracie's is an odd place—not much laughing like at Arnie's. I've only gone there to be alone, having found it once while looking for a greasy spoon to get a bite on the way home from a night call-in at St. Francis. Gracie's is hidden at the end of a strip mall. Hard to see how it could have enough business to survive. There is a different clientele, most of them alone, avoiding each other's glances, a place where introverts, pedophiles, wife-beaters, and socially inept left-overs go to be anonymous, which is why I was there that night. Not many tables or stools were vacant.

"Sometime during showering, eating spaghetti, running the safety code to access the weapon, to the cold beer at Gracie's, my internal committee had ruled. The target would be Joe; failing that, it might be myself. My life was complete—duty to country, even if unnoticed; duty to family, all insured; duty to work. And I was still just an angry SOB. I really can't tell you why I decided on one round in that Luger, locked and tucked in the back of my waist, except to force a decision on myself. In the Navy, and after, I had given what I could give. So now, as a last full measure of devotion, I would expunge a scourge from my family and community, or leave the stage and let other harpies do the job. The only question left was why was I still at Gracie's? After the fourth tall one, and a last satisfyingly long piss, I navigated my way through and around the tables and chairs of the sad and lost who shared my invisible existence, past the smoked-glass door to the parking lot."

AJ chuckled softly, tilted his head and grinned at Miko. "But then, in my infinite wisdom, more questions arose, like where the fuck are my keys? How the fuck did I get here on this curb? How the fuck did these two patrol cars get here, and why is my weapon being handled by one of the officers, another flipping through my wallet? That noise turned out to be radio chatter, and the strobe from the cherry-top was also keeping me awake. My hearing improved by the dulling of other senses—I could hear the cops' chatter from about ten yards away. 'Yeah, this is Jimmy's buddy, the one whose wife called Jimmy. Yeah, that's the one—no telling what he was up to. We're calling in a drunk call with self-harm risk, so back up is taking him to the Public Health over in their precinct, since he's a vet. So, hey, listen up, that other gig is off for tonight.'

"And that's the whole sad story of how you, young man, got stuck with me!"

"Few things are black and white, are they, AJ?" Miko noted. "Where are we now?"

AJ stretched his arms and legs without rising and sighed. "Well, since then, you're right. I did contact that district attorney. The legal prosecution process takes forever, but the bank audit led to the state's attorney getting involved anyway. Long and short of it, over the past year, step-by-step, since I was admitted here, evidence was accumulated for a lock-tight case against Joe, and against my sister as an accomplice. It went to criminal court over the last few months. Joe was remanded to a prison in Florida to be incarcerated for six months—the rest of a two-year sentence on house arrest. Karli got six months house arrest. There was no money left to recover, although it seems a couple of their sons may have squirreled some of it away to banks in Buenos Aires." AJ broke into a sarcastic grin. "And I'm still not in jail, so I guess you are right, Dr. Smartass.

Calling the DA would have been the right course to take in the first place."

"Hmm." Miko smiled. "Some of us piss-ants get a lot of schooling to make up for inexperience. It's a trade-off." Miko logged in and gave AJ a card for their next scheduled visit. "You've made good progress since that night, AJ, even if you wanted to beat me up for ripping the scab off a wound."

"Well, guess I can't change overnight." AJ admitted. "And hey, sorry for my outburst. At least, maybe I'm getting better at apologizing. Anyway, you seem to be able to take quite a bit without losing your shit. Maybe I'll try to follow your example."

CHAPTER 25
RESOLUTION

"**M**any memories have faded, but this one will not," the old man mumbled as his grandson supported him across the threshold. The grandson, who politely introduced himself as Adrian Demaris, knew that the odor of the unwashed, stooped gentleman would not go unnoticed. Miko could not dismiss the unmistakable shit-sweet hint of melena, the black, tarry effluent of stool mixed with decomposing blood, signaling that for any number of reasons, the old man's days may well be numbered.

"Are you related to Demetrius Constantine?" the old man asked in a high, raspy voice.

Miko and Sophia glanced at each other. The mens' appearance at Sophia's door had taken them out of their conversation about Miko's hopeful interviews, speculating how his transition back from the States in six months might pan out.

Miko took charge, as his mother's blank expression indicated she was still sorting, not knowing whether to answer this stranger. "Yes," Miko replied, deploying his calming physician voice. "Demetrius was this woman's father and my own grandfather. Did you know him? He is more than twenty years passed away. Why you are here?"

Adrian kept silent, though his mouth remained slightly open as if prepared at any moment to fill in for his grandfather's stumbling introduction.

Sophia responded to Miko's less suspicious lead, quickly procuring a sturdy wooden chair, and beckoned the ancient and vulnerable stranger to sit, before going on. The grandson carefully lowered him to the seat, supporting his descent from the front with both arms in a maneuver that appeared well practiced. The old man took several long breaths to recover, laying his inauspicious wooden cane across his lap.

"I don't have much time, and I am weak," he began. "Seaman Constantine saved my life. He saved all of us. I thought he must have gone down with the ship, but there was a rumor some years ago that he did not. I've had a long life, as you can see, heh, heh," the old seaman shared in a wheezy scoff. "Nobody said anything about it. The ship was lost, and I suppose that these things seem so minor in that situation. But there must have been twenty of us who got out because Papagiannis stayed and got the hatch open as she went down. I . . . I . . . ," he paused, as if a rush of thoughts had befuddled the story he had come prepared to tell. "Now I'm confused, and don't know what to say," looking to his grandson for support.

Adrian drew a long breath and cleared his throat gently. "I'm sorry, this is my grandfather, Mr. Petri Demaris. Please forgive the intrusion, but he wanted so badly to meet you. My grandfather was a sailor in the Royal Navy when he was eighteen. He has told us a story many times over the years that in the Second World War his ship was sinking after being bombed by the Germans. Hatches in compartments were closed to maintain buoyancy. Papa here was in the engine compartment. Somehow, at the last minute, another sailor opened the hatch to that compartment, and all the men in the engine room got out with moments to spare, before it would have been too late. The ship went down, taking many other souls. Some of my grandfather's shipmates who survived have talked over the years about who the sailor was who opened the hatch, because he could have gotten himself killed by staying that long. Somehow, they deduced it must have been Demetrius Constantine. There is probably no military documentation of anything from that time, but my grandfather, please excuse us, he couldn't be persuaded to let this possibility go."

Miko and Sophia looked at each other again. Sophia's gaze went to the floor. "My father never talked to us about the war. We thought he was ashamed that it went badly for the navy at the beginning."

"It was disaster!" the old man hissed. "We were crushed. We were all ashamed and had no one to tell. We all kept silent for too long." His voice had begun to quake.

"I should get him back to the car and home soon," the grandson interjected. "My grandfather wanted to say thank you to the family of Demetrius Constantine, if he could. My grandfather, well," the grandson hesitated, "We all love him. He has given us all a good life, but this thing from the war, before all of us, he wanted to say something. He would not rest. One of the other families thought Mr. Constantine or his family might be at this house."

The old man's face had grown tight, lips pursed, eyes filled with ageless tears. As he was supported to his feet again, he wiped his face with a bare hand, then his coat sleeve. He smiled gently, and drew a long sigh, as one having laid down a burden. "No one can pay this back. They can only remember. Now you must remember. Thank you," the man said, reaching for Sophia's hand, then Miko's shoulder. "Goodbye now," he said, already in a shuffling turn toward the door.

"Thank you for coming," Miko replied. Sophia stood silent, her eyes wetting and wide. They watched the old man manage his passage through the door, carefully, though slightly more upright than upon his entry.

As the light through the door closed to darken the small foyer where they had clustered, Sophia stared toward the floor in front of her to the infinity seen in the absence of light.

"Wow, Momma, I can feel my heart beating faster. Are you okay?" Miko dragged one of the kitchen chairs, and positioned himself at an angle facing her, reflexively reaching for her pulse. "That was so strange! What did you think about what Mr. Demaris said about Grampa? Do you believe it?"

"I didn't know what to ask." Her eyes rose to meet Miko's. "That sailor who opened the hatch could have been anyone. After all these years, how could it be known? But, yes, somehow, I believe it is probably true. It is too strange to be made up."

"That's one way to look at it. But why wouldn't Grampa tell us that story—that he saved someone, or even a lot of guys?"

Now the blossoming psychiatrist and the widow slipped back to the roles where she was mother and teacher, and he was son and student. Alone now, there was no one to tease them about it, and both relished that they could lovingly still play at it. Lunch would pass contemplatively at the same table where, in this dynamic, inspirations had been passed long ago.

Sophia's belated answer had formulated during the light meal. "Heroes don't see their acts as heroic, they see them as obligations, and they just do what they have to do. I imagine your grandfather would be embarrassed if he talked about maybe saving some guys when so many others died. And no one wanted to hear such stories then. People naturally want to hear sweet things or nothing at all. My mother said she and Demetrius just wanted to get on after the war, but the war always stayed with him. Silently. It lived as a ghost, moving and followed him to all the rooms, always not far behind." She paused, brushing a few crumbs from her lap. "Now we have something more to think about."

Miko smiled at his mother as he rose. It was the smile she'd seen when he was processing a pronouncement from Momma, not yet sure whether to accept or dismiss her premise.

"Okay," Miko slapped his palms together in determination. "I'm going to go through my room, and get the stuff sorted. I can probably get all the junk in one plastic bag."

"Take the bag," she agreed, "But look at everything carefully and don't throw anything out until I check everything."

It was not like her to hover about throwing out junk, he puzzled, but agreed to be circumspect.

The effort began with an eye for expediency in weeding through his long neglected and unnecessary possessions. As he stood slowly scanning the room, organizing zeal gave way to the angles and textures that had framed and possessed his thoughtful adolescence. These traces called him softly to the safe house of his imagination, the daydreams and night dreams for which he had an instinctive passion and penchant for painting in words. People had once read them and been moved or at least puzzled. Indeed, the years away had begun when he was finishing middle school. By then it was no longer the right atmosphere, almost embarrassing, to bring his adolescing friends into the sanctum—all gibbering in boyish rebellion, all turning by then from imagination to boasting what they would do and be in the future. The smell of the plaster and old timber, the light shaft through the window, the slant of the ceiling over the single bed, and the creak from the oak floor near the middle of it were as a portrait, just out of reach, and remaining. A few model boats, a deflated FIFA regulation football, a few novels and picture books, yearbooks, binders kept from courses that felt pivotal to him at some time—all had their position here without ranking. Things kept from one moment of value and displaced by the next.

The notebook on the shelf over the window beckoned, sirening its primacy in this mindless moment of presence. This may be worth looking at, for his best treasures had been inserted there, qualifying for inclusion, each by holding a complete thought in a story of some sort, written by the boy who wandered away to become a man. The notebook, once protected by being relatively out of reach and out of sight to probing friends who might tease, was easy to reach now by the adult. He settled into the barely adequate chair at the desk. As if to an aging lover, he gave the notebook a patient smile and turned the cover, ready to dwell for a time with his self in the age of wonder, each entry a tale to warm one's soul on an inclement night.

His back straightened at the first single page in the note-book, loose and out of place. His hand stretched it out into the filamentous glare of the sunbeam through the window. It was not his writing. Legible, yet unfamiliar, his eyes slipped quickly to the bottom for the credit. Kostas? His papa? How had something written by his father, if indeed it were him, made it to his childhood notebook? Miko scooted the chair slightly toward the shaft of light, holding it with both hands, briefly smoothing the creases of its folds. His father's hand-writing showed no timidity, the dark bold ink nearly lifting from the white paper in its spotlight.

Sophia, my love,

You know I don't pray much, but I ask God now that you find this letter at a time when you will best understand. The things I want to say, well, I wish I had our son's way with words. I am at peace with my choices, mostly the joy of having you in my life. What more could a man have? You must then know the what and the why when God says it is time.

What? The back pain that has taken my sleep and hunger away is from cancer. The doctors tell me it started in my pancreas but is now everywhere. They say there are medicines and big surgeries that may give me a little more time, maybe not much. Soon I would be getting sicker and sicker. It would be hard for you and Miko.

You have been my life's love and joy. The sea has been my life's work. It is in me already. I have taken from it every day and now I will give back. They will think I have been robbed and killed in these troubled times. You will get the full pension and keep all that we have saved up to now without my illness draining it. It must be our secret what I do today, or I fear the pension may be less if they know. You should know only after, or you will not permit my decision.

I have been carrying Demetrius's pistol for protection, and now it will free me. Selene will be very low on petrol. I will lock her into sharp starboard turn, and she will circle hard until she is exhausted. The pistol will be tied to my wrist and fall with me, the irons on a rope hanging from my middle over port side that bring me lifeless to the deep in a moment. I will be fish food, ha-ha! I think Selene will be found adrift before much damage as clear skies and calm seas are predicted this week. She should bring a good price for you.

Why? I accept my time is now. You will be better off not seeing me slowly waste to dust. Miko will not be confused about what he should do in this situation. It is my last act of responsibility to the two I love most in the world. I am not sad. Do not be sad yourself. I know your goodness and your strength.

If a good man has you after me, you are your own to give. It would not make me nor us anything less.

Maybe you will find this letter today, maybe a long time from now. No matter. It will be the right time for you. Tell Miko if it helps.

All my love, Kostas

Moisture formed on his chin and brow as Miko became aware of the steady hammering in his chest for the second time today. The paper's subtle rippling belied the fine tremor in his hands. He looked left and right into corners of the room blackened by the visual effects of the glaring white he had been focused on. Was that a gunshot he had heard, or did he imagine it? By the third reading, the pieces of the undated writing were coming together. Why and when would this suicide note, if it were real, be placed in his childhood notebook? His investigative impulses began to melt into the larger meanings of why. What did it all say about his father? What did it say about Miko's responsibility, so devastating, psychologically, to himself, and so misplaced in the context of his father's reality. What did Momma know?

He placed the letter flat on the obscured desk, wiped clammy palms on his pant legs, folded the letter, quickly placed it in the notebook, and returned the notebook to its former berth over the window, restoring the world, for the moment, to its former order. Sitting again, he continued to wipe hands on clothes nervously. There was no approved solution to how he would bring this to his Momma.

"Momma," Miko's voice cracked, and he quickly cleared his throat, and called to the kitchen again. "Momma, could you come here for a minute, to my room?"

He waited, leaning out the doorway to hear or see her approaching. Head tilted questioningly, she strode toward him with a gentle smile, drying her hands on her apron. "Yes, dear, what is it? Have you found a treasure from the past?"

Miko sniffed deeply, his tension released a bit in the irony. "Yes, something from the past." He returned her smile, already noting his internal detente and submission to the moment. Motioning her to the bed, he gestured her to sit, as he resettled into the chair. Moment by moment, the course of the afternoon sun was bringing a broader illumination to the quarters.

Her eyes fixed on Miko's, as his gaze moved aimlessly about before settling back on her. He rose, turned, and reached again for the notebook.

"You found the letter so quickly," she said softly, and froze Miko's motion with the notebook still over his head. "It's good." Sophia judged confidently. "Now we can talk."

Miko settled again into the desk chair, slump-shouldered, expression drained from his face, the notebook lighting squarely on his lap. "How long have you known this, Momma?"

"I'm not a suspicious person, but I'm not blind. Your Papa's mood that morning, setting out as if he had not a care in the world, not sick, just another day at fishing. When the boat was found, and not a trace of him except blood, I wondered. Kostas had asked me, before his goodbye kiss that day, to look after your room, but I put it off and never wondered why he brought up such a stupid thing. Until one day, after your last time here, missing you, missing him, I needed comfort, and thought I would find it in your simple stories. I found you both again." Her voice spiraled as she pushed back the rising bittersweet memory of the moment. "I found the letter at a good time for me," she said, quickly regaining her composure. "I wanted you to find it in the same way, to have you hear it from your papa, alone." Sofia searched Miko's soft, expressionless face and motionless form, framed within the light and shadows, the notebook now embraced gently to his chest. "Do not judge your papa," she murmured. "I do not. He was the finest man I ever knew. No surprises. Nothing for himself. You are older now, Miko. Can you understand all this?"

Miko's boyhood innocence had long ago dissipated. He had found in the domain of medicine a cruel mistress, one that offers hope to a mortal species. He lived face-to-face with the eternal paradox of his labor. The chief of service had told the residents on more than one occasion that doctrine, guidelines, and ideology remain suggestions, while cold reality, when one must take a critical decision, forces one to gather and to synthesize all facts available in the moment, then act. Physicians are fundamentally taught to approach suicide as a failure of care, a failure of the patient and their support systems, a failure of physicians to find the right coping strategy. "Harming no other, we have a right to our own rationale in the face of all persuasion," the chief would say. "Only the timing of our deaths is shifted, not the certainty." Here it was, at Miko's own doorstep.

Not fully rising, Miko transferred to sit beside his mother, their sideways embrace releasing long-withheld soft shudders and the flow of grieving. His breathing slowly returned to normal cadence. Sophia straightened him at the shoulders and cupped his face in her hands.

"I love you, my son, the doctor!" she said with a satisfied smile. "I'll let you finish your task here. There are no more secrets." She turned back to him at the door. "Once, when you were little, I asked you to explain your grandfather's grumpiness to me if you ever could. See how smart I am! Now you are a doctor, and you talk to many grumpy old soldiers. You should be able to talk about your grandfather, now that we have heard that he was not so bad!"

CHAPTER 26

THE TALK

Miko's emergence from processing through arrival at Tulsa International approached midnight, following the three-lay-over itinerary from Athens. Bia struggled to stifle her yawns on meeting him outside baggage claim.

"How was your flight, love?" She caught herself using the language of their earlier times and looked to see if he noticed the slip.

"Bia, let me drive home." Miko took her hand as he raised his head to peer along the conveyor for the roller bag he had checked on the last leg. She noticed unexpected energy in his response. "We need to talk."

"But you must be exhausted!" She knew she was speaking for herself, now at the end of a week of emotional preparation for the unavoidable discussion that loomed. His resoluteness, she figured, could only be a signal that he was ready to take the necessary steps. "Can it wait?" Bia importuned. The nausea that had accompanied her morning squeamishness, even for coffee, had lingered today, worryingly amplified with the late hour and her dread. In whatever way he would leave her, and for whom, didn't seem to matter now. In the pall of night, the layers of complexity that would be surreal in bright day, now seemed sadly laughable.

"Well, I'd rather not," he replied coyly. "Besides, we'll both probably sleep better if I get some things off my chest. Let's get through the toll gate first."

Bia nodded. In the active silence, she would work out her approach.

The highway was virtually empty at that hour as Miko negotiated the series of interchanges before I-40 put them on the glide toward center city. "Bia, I need to explain some things . . ."

"Me first!" Bia cut him off, unapologetically. "I might be able to spare you any long explanations, Miko," she huffed. "Not to spoil your party, but I'm pregnant. It's my fault; I missed a few days at the end of my cycle, and there you go." Bia surprised herself with her own boldness. "I'll just have it taken care of, and we can get on with the divorce, and you can have Dr. what's-her-name, and I'll go back home." Staring out into the dark-light waves flowing from the passing freeway lamps helped her composure. She had already played out in her head his lame narrative —'we were too young; I've entered a new life and found myself and it doesn't include you; I've fallen in love with someone who shares a professional outlook like mine.' She would cut it off before it gets to the sad 'I just don't love you anymore.'

"You're pregnant!" came the question as an exclamation. He quickly checked his mirrors and surroundings to make an unplanned stop.

Bia noted more mellow than drama in Miko's surprise. She cringed at his dopey, wide-eyed, open-mouth face as he maneuvered off the next exit and toward an empty space in the Denny's parking lot. She would keep that goofy image of him in mind forever to convince her that divorce was the only reasonable thing. The clownishness of the bright lights and signs of the ubiquitous nighttime food haven would add the perfect condiment to the vulgarity in this moment of exposure, she thought.

"You're pregnant?" Again, she thought she heard glee, not sarcasm in Miko's dumb repetition. "And what are you talking about? Dr. Who?"

"Miko, it's no mystery. We don't talk about us anymore. It's all about your job, my job, money. This is not what we said we would do. I think you have emotionally moved on from me and see a better future for yourself. I get it. Let's not make this any worse than it has to be."

Bia watched Miko's face traverse wordlessly through befuddlement, surprise, wonder, joy, analysis, and back again. That this was not the discussion he was expecting was little consolation to her. His capitulation was unexpected.

Still, the flustered man stared at her, then back to the steering wheel, repeatedly, slack-jawed. Bia squinted suspiciously in the flaky lighting. Miko held his lips pursed. He folded his hands in his lap, head down as he began. "We now have more to talk about than I realized," he remarked, wading in. "On the contrary, please, let me be the one to save you any long explanations, if possible. Can you be patient with me for just a minute?"

Bia tilted her head in the same 'I'm listening, and this better be good' position that Miko had more than once described his mother using.

Miko paused. She was acquainted with the tactics he had learned from professors, including the pause to gain attention. She was not inclined to be patient.

"I believe there is a mechanism within all of us that resorts to blaming when we can't accept our own weakness and failures," Miko began. "I fell in love with you and somewhere along the line, I conjured up a scenario where you were to blame for my turning to medicine and not writing like I thought I would do from the beginning. I thought I needed to be something more honorable, that I needed to make steady income to take care of you. Hell, this is the twenty-first century, and I would still use those old constructs to make my case against you. I did not discuss it with you; if I did, you would have so easily destroyed the myth I've been telling myself. I built a wall. It was easy to do because I was already angry with myself for not being there when we thought my father was murdered, that I had strayed from his life, from writing, from Momma, all the things that were important to me. So selfishly! You were here, so I made you the selfish one. Now you live with a grumpy young man, like my grandfather was the old grumpy man in our lives when I was little. The last thing I could imagine was being someone like him, and it's what I've become, wrapped up in my imaginary transgressions. Am I making any sense?"

"No, but go on," Bia puzzled, whiffing that he was intellectualizing and blowing smoke. It didn't make sense, she thought, but, on the other hand, it felt like they might be talking.

Miko swallowed hard and spoke haltingly. "Wow, the last few days have been full of surprises. I . . . I found out my father was not murdered, and I could not have saved him. My father died of pancreatic cancer; he chose to end that tragedy on his own terms to protect my mother, as always. I found out that the mean old man in my memory, my grandfather, was probably some kind of war hero, and probably no different from the vets I see at work. And because of those vets, I was able to give my mother some understanding of what happens to young men in war that changes them. I've been closing myself off from you, because I had closed off from myself."

Miko looked up from his hands to Bia's waiting eyes. "I'm sorry," he droned. "How could you stand it?"

Bia sat up straight and pressed her head backward into the headrest, stretching her tense shoulders and neck. The detour from the confrontation she had been expecting had jolted her more alert despite the exhaustion. What happened to the other woman, she thought. The papa, the grandpa, the loss of himself—what were these dimensions of the Miko she thought she knew? Words came from nowhere, unleashed from a dam of pent-up fears.

"Because . . . ," Bia sobbed openly, "Because I've been so afraid I lost you to someone or something else, and I had faded from you somewhere along the road to your future. She massaged her forehead with her fingertips for a moment, and crossed her arms. "I guess, in a way, I made you the bad guy as well," Bia sighed.

"Well, I'm not going anywhere." Miko chided. "If you leave, I'm going to chase you and this child all around the world. And I'm a psychiatrist. I know how stalkers think!"

"But, who . . . ?" Bia paused, shifting to neutral in her seat, forehead wrinkled, eyes straining into the black, wet night. Her own capitulation was on the edge—one smoldering ember left to be doused. "Who is the red-haired woman. I saw you and her; you embraced her, and I know tenderness when I see it. You walked with her, and you met her at the coffee shop."

"What woman!" Miko almost shouted into the enclosed space, eyes and mouth agape, palms opened upward, completing the caricature of exasperation.

"She dresses in very good taste." Bia added the final clue.

The caricature collapsed, leaving Miko's chin on his chest. "Oh my god! Nora? She's one of the other foreign medical graduates. She's Dutch." Miko then mustered a sheepish smile. "Yes, well, Nora is quite attractive, and more, she has brains that burn and she comes from a wealthy family in Maastricht."

"What are you doing?" Bia already sensed a ruse.

"Nora has met a challenge. She's one of those exceptionally brilliant people who excel in medical school and then has difficulty connecting with patients—like a phobia for examining strangers. She's very sweet and coming to terms with the value of a career in not-so-touchy areas like pathology, bench research, imaging, and so forth. She's afraid to disappoint her father who is a respected oncologist in the Netherlands. A group of us have been letting her vent. She's turned the corner, and she's found a new love in cancer immunohistochemistry research. Mid-year, she's transferring to the Cleveland Clinic. She just needed a little affirmation from her peers. Sometimes the passage seems all laid out, then you hit a curve. I know what that feels like."

"Oh, hell!" Bia scoffed, blowing her nose on a spare Subway napkin from the glove box, then wadding and throwing it at him. "I don't know whether to slap you or to hug you!" Bia said flatly, keeping her guard up. "We might as well get some coffee and breakfast while we're here. I haven't eaten well in days. Now I'm starving!"

Approaching the garish light of the eternal diner, she took his hand in both of hers, and pulled him hard to her side, almost tripping the two of them. "My baby will need a papa like your Papa. Don't forget that!" she said sternly. "Do you still want to do psychiatry, or will you go back to trying to be a writer and starve us? Or will you finally live an honest life as fisherman like your Papa? Make up your mind!"

Miko stopped just before the lighting intensified near the restaurant doors and faced Bia. The laugh she expected had been shanghaied by unexpected solemness.

"I'm exactly where I should be, Bia," Miko reported sharply. "I'm here. I'm here to understand and to write about the psychological impact of war on soldiers and sailors through their stories. And now, I'm going to be a father."

The rain had stopped, and the new quiet dawned on the them at the same moment. In sync, they turned slowly and resumed a slower pace to the entrance.

"Okay, Mr. Doctor-Writer," Bia joked, as Miko drew the door open for her, "then you should begin with some creative thinking on baby names!"

"Be with you in a second, folks," the waiter chimed as the couple slid into the booth.

"I think you liked my Papa, and for good reason," Miko began filling the silence. "How about 'Kostas' if it's a boy, and 'Selene' if it's a girl?"

"*Selene*, like your papa's boat? I have always liked that name, simple and elegant. Yes—I like them both," Bia's melodic voice reinfusing. "So what will you write next, then?"

"Well, that's another piece of good news. The chief has been pleased with my work in the VA side of clinic. Already he has suggested that the senior residents compile a manual of approaches to psychiatric management related to veterans, you know, a sort of specialty manual for career people, fashioned off the work over the past few decades in other special populations. I was in his office to remind him of my vacation absence and who would be covering the clinic and wards, and this idea just came up. We chatted for a while. I just mentioned that I once thought of being a writer in a different way, and he said I should think about taking the lead as first author and editor. And you know, I got so excited, I started writing on the flight back. I was so into composing a draft for a preface, I almost missed one of my connections. I want you to read it. It's very rough, so far. You can be my first proofreader and critic! The chief wants the manuscript completed by the end of my senior year. Look, I'll show you," Miko's voice drew attention from other diners, as he withdrew a couple of crumpled pages from his pants pocket. Bia shushed him gently with hand motions and took the pages.

"The psycho-emotional effects of war are varied, both at the categorical level and at the individual level, but they are universal in combat veterans of all services and theaters.

Their intensity and character of features vary in the amount of carnage and cruelty witnessed, and the amount of personal loss of close friends. The moral injury occurs to our fellow human beings—men and women who leave their natural family and must quickly find a new family whose bonds rule over life and death. Within those acquired families, both the interdependence and the sense of purpose and personal worth are amplified to a level that may never be experienced again, leaving the soldier or sailor feeling that the rest of life is a pale shadow of these young years. With each combat experience, each day of survival, each kill, each accomplished mission, each loss, the combatant creates their war garment. It is the black and white armor of kill or be killed, of kill every enemy to save one comrade. Some can don and doff this garment; some wear it always and forever, never feeling quite safe again without it. Mercenaries are born in this domain and will die off or age out. Unmanaged or managed poorly, as is so often the case, transitions back to regular life can be disastrous. Society plays a critical role in that management by the way we receive our warriors home, honorable in duty and courage, regardless of the political mood of our country.

"It does not have to be this way. As long as there is military conflict and open war, we must develop a trauma-informed care plan for each and every soldier and sailor, tailored to their needs. Consistent application of these plans must be a fundamental and adequate category of the defense budget.

"Our medications may help in some measure with symptoms. The images burned into the neural patterns, however, are not easily excised, purged, or dulled. The brain's neuroplasticity after neurotrauma holds promise of a coming era of therapies to rewire both movement and emotional responses. In the meantime, we can give the images an emotional and psychological room of their own, and a purpose, while mediating in a harm reduction framework. The room the images occupy must be made habitable with the telling and the acceptance of what they are, while not allowed to occupy the other rooms in the mind. There are shelves in this room to store the real and perceived brutality and atrocities individually, collectively, and mutually committed; shelves for the pain of the losses never forgotten; shelves for the real and perceived failures in the fog of war, and shelves for the fear and moments of cowardice that all people have. They must keep company with the honors of remembrance. The veteran must be shown how to let others see into the room, acknowledge its occupants, and aerate the room from time to time to prevent the house from exploding. It is a repetitive process. Indeed, it is a family process, as with other chronic afflictions, to keep us close and reduce harm to all involved with their care.

"I am grateful to the veterans I've met who have provided our psychiatry community new perspectives and tools with which to engage these issues, not only for themselves and other vets, but for battered and abused persons in many circumstances and conditions."

Bia peered into Miko's eyes. "I may not understand all the English, so don't be too proud." She looked down at the pages she held and back again and reached for Miko's hand. "Please, stop doubting yourself. Let this work be your work. Let me be your partner. It's good we can talk again."

CHAPTER 27

THE FALL

The moment before impact seemed to linger in his recollection, the second or two between one recognizing they're in trouble, and its consequences. The surgical neck of the femur, the closest part of the hip bone, fractured through and through with the impact of the full body weight on the concrete, unconstrained from the full four-foot distance where his feet had just been, and seven feet from the hip's previous altitude. Never had he experienced such an intense blow— not from a punch nor from walking into someone's swinging softball bat. The sound of bone breaking, knowing it is one's own, feeling the stun and sting of the first pain, knowing one can't take it back, all collide. As the muscles of the region are recruited to immobilize the faller, it is a half-minute before the body punishes any attempt to rise, roll, or drag by meting out breath-taking, shuddering shocks of pain. AJ retraced the thoughtless path to that moment of realization that he had entered a place foreign to him.

One two-foot artificial Christmas tree had been over-looked on the previous afternoon, when he had retrieved the bulk of the decorations. He'd get this one as well, to please

Natalia. Knowing better, he went to the fully enclosed garage half-alert, still in his skivvies and flip-flops. He scaled the ladder, drew out the missing ornament reachable along the dark inner angle of the attic, with only his head and chest through the hatch. Catching the heel of one flip-flop on the first descending rung was all that was needed to tip his now stunned corpus into free-fall, one hand ejecting the soulless adornment, while the other arm extended reflexively to break the fall. The first moment of recumbency set his conscious self-criticism underway, interrupted the next moment by a sense of tightening in his left thigh and buttock, as blood and body fluid oozed surreptitiously into muscle and connective tissues. The skin of the thigh and groin were soon rendered taut in an insidious march toward gross swelling. Any attempt at repositioning was futile, castigated by another nauseating, exquisite bolt of pain. He lay motionless, hoping some aspect of this would eventually pass and he could get himself up, alone. He lay for twenty minutes, aware of every second.

"Natalia!" he shouted, stifled, lest a greater burst of air provoke another jolt of lancinating pain. The washer cycle had stopped; the renewed quiet should allow the call to reach her. It did.

"Oh my god, AJ, what happened!" she said, scanning the scene where the ladder still stood precariously half-cocked through the ceiling hatch, AJ's gritting face half-turned to the cold pavement.

"What's it look like?" he barked in frustration. "I caught my god-damned flip-flop on the ladder and lost my balance." She could hear his voice beginning to crack and tighten. "I can't move—ow, ow, ow, ow, ow, fuck!" he shouted, his shoulders shuddering, followed by retching with nothing to show for it before breakfast.

"Let me call an ambulance to get you to the hospital. You probably broke your leg."

"I don't need to go to the hospital. Just help me up!"

"I'm not strong enough to lift you, AJ. Are you crazy? That might hurt you more. At least let me call Tony over. He knows how to move injured people in the ER."

Facial sweat had pooled on the garage floor. Natalia quickly gathered a blanket from a storage cabinet and covered him, tucking around his contact points with the floor as gently as possible to avoid unintentional movement. She didn't stare as he tried to grimace back tears and moans. She changed the blanket after he could no longer hold urine or stool back. She had never seen him so helpless and dependent, even in his most drunken stupor, and even embarrassed, an emotion that he had little notion of.

"I'm going to pack your leg in ice where it hurts the most to slow the swelling, but we'll still try to keep you warm."

"Don't be stupid," AJ barked. "I'm already freezing!"

The retort stung, as so many had over so many years of criticism. Fluidly and calmly going about as if this were routine childcare, an unfamiliar voice arose in Natalia's head. "You son-of-a-bitch! I'm so glad to see you suffer the way you've made me and the kids suffer, and god knows who else! God damn you, you big fucking asshole! You're finally getting a taste of what you deserve! See what it feels like to be helpless and brutalized? I should just go shopping and leave you here to rot, you bastard!"

She turned away from AJ, hand over mouth, lest those words escape. Tears welled up at the possibility that a brethren demon might possess her, as it so often had possessed him. How could she be that way? How could either of them be that way? She had developed a sensitized nose for the essence of booze, often cleverly hidden in the garage. The atmosphere about him registered none.

"AJ, I know you're in a lot of pain, and how hard it is for you to accept help. But right now, honey, I'm all you've got! So here's the plan. Listen to me. I'm going to get you warmed up and maybe a bit more relaxed. Let's try to get a little coffee into you and maybe a snack. Then we're going to try to roll you over flat on that old dry, comfy quilt. I can't lift you, but I think I can sort of drag you over the threshold into the laundry room. I'm going to get you cleaned up there, and we'll try to get you into a pair of clean shorts and some kind of shirt. You can pee in a bottle if you need to. And when that's settled, I'm going to call Tony over here. Remember your son Tony, the ER nurse!" she delivered sarcastically. "It'll take fifteen minutes, no more. And if he agrees from a professional point of view, I'm going to call for hospital transport. That's what we're doing. We can't stay like this. It's not an option."

AJ's affirmative nod signaled that he was beaten. When these steps were taken, she would wash, at least her face and hands, of the cruel schadenfreude she had met within.

CHAPTER 28

RESURRECTION

Jostled by the nurse and the aid shifting his position with a pull sheet, AJ awoke to a mouth parched by morphine, the ultimate release from his agony. The relief came at the expense of a clouded sensorium and no recollection of how he had gotten here—in traction with an IV—finally warm and toasty, freed somehow from the garage's concrete slab.

"Nurse, can I have some water? Whoa, my mouth is so dry!"

Without answering, the slight, wide-smiled Filipino LPN first lifted the Foley bag above the bed level for a measurement of urinary output. "Well, look at that! Much less concentrated now. Mr. AJ, through your IV, we've already gotten in three of the six liters of fluid the surgeon wants before your fixation in the morning. You're doing good! How is your pain?"

AJ bathed in the calm, vague sense of numbness all over, a bit amazed of the effectiveness of the narcotic. "Good, good, okay. Is that from what I'm getting in the IV? Oh, and can I get something to drink?"

"Doctor has you on morphine for the pain, and you let me know if it gets bad again." She bounced up on her tiptoes to bring her face closer to his for better communication. "You'll want to relax the muscles, too. Relaxing the muscles and the traction will help line up your bones for fixation in the morning. Sorry, only ice chips and glycerin swabs for your dry mouth; also from the pain medicine. Stomach must be empty when you go to surgery."

"Doctor? Who's the doctor? Is my wife here somewhere?" AJ slurred.

"Doctor Hofstadter your doctor. Very good orthopedist here. He talked to your wife when she was here. She's gone now and will come in before your surgery in the morning. Ooh, she was so tired by the time she left! She needed some sleep herself. She and your son got you here in ambulance. Did good job, too. Like a pro. You're a lucky man. Very nice lady!"

"Hofstadter? David Hofstadter?" AJ had played with the men's softball team before retirement. The corporate league had been a great equalizer among the hospitals, physicians, executives, and other staff. AJ remembered Hofstadter as a power hitter, but slow around the bases, with a truculent demeanor that improved the longer he was outdoors and on the field. They had won many games together. Hofstadter was notorious for his goofy jig when they did.

Still in a morphine trance at 0600, AJ awoke to the surgeon's round face inches from his. "Hey, AJ, you sorry sack of shit, now even I'm going to be able to outrun you! How're you feeling? Ready to get fixed up? If we can do this all with screws and a small plate, and I think we can, you'll be better off in the long run over a replacement. It's a fairly clean break across the neck of the femur; the head and socket are not involved. Do you have any questions before the anesthesiologist puts you out? I've filled Natalia in as well—she's just outside pre-op. We've got a couple of units of blood on standby if things get iffy. Your cardiologist has been alerted and given the go ahead and will follow-up this afternoon."

"David, I thought my wife would at least get me a real doctor, but I guess she hates me that much," AJ mumbled in submission.

"Hey, sucker, from the story I heard, it sounds to me like that woman did everything right. Had she not been there and did what she did, just good common-sense first-aid, you know, an old dipshit like you may have bled half your volume into that thigh, gone into shock, and you could have found yourself dead on your own fucking garage floor. How long you guys been married? Hey, if you don't survive now, can I have her?" The large, cartoonishly grinning surgeon cracked himself up. "Count your blessings, dummy! I'll tell you more later when you're awake again. Oh, and wish me luck. I've always wanted to do one of these! Nighty-night!"

Through the haze, AJ had a single, fleeting, clear thought: how well Hofstadter had pegged him. The sarcastic banter comforted more than any medical jargon could. He knew he'd be alright. Confidence and competence may sound different to a combat veteran, even still. The surgeon saw him as he was. AJ drifted seamlessly under as the comments about Natalia's actions lingered.

Ψ

The bacon and coffee smelled irresistible and belied their bland presentation on a hospital tray. AJ focused on them as a nurse-figure hovered about, straightening bedding, getting vitals, and measuring fluid output.

"Good! It's about time you eat better!" the hoverer commented. "Today we'll get you up after breakfast. You'll get started with PT."

"That sounds good." AJ mumbled. "This damn leg is pretty sore, but it feels like I need to stretch." The women moved into focus. "Are all the nurses here Filipino?" he asked, still disinhibited from the meds.

"Mostly. But me, I'm Vietnamese. I'm from Ho Chi Minh City. You know it? The money is better here. Do you not like the Vietnamese? Many old men here say bad things about Vietnamese," she replied, glancing for his reaction.

"I got no problem with that." AJ paused, deciding not to bring up the war. "Thanks for helping me. The chow smells good." AJ watched the petite whirlwind moving efficiently from straightening bed clothes, to checking the IV site, the Foley urinary tube and bag, and the vitals. "How long was I out?"

"What do you mean?" She stopped.

"How long was I in surgery this morning?" AJ clarified.

The nurse smiled widely. "Your surgery was three days ago! You did fine—usual time, no complications, but you got four units from blood bank. You needed lots of pain meds. Guess you don't remember a lot, but it's good to see you asking questions and hungry. Good progress."

"Are you kidding? Last thing I remember is talking with the surgeon before I went in. Guess it did go well, huh!"

"Like I said, no other problems." She plumped his pillows behind him. "And your wife understands what your schedule will be like when you go home—PT, follow-up, medications. She's a smart woman. You'll be in good hands. You better keep her happy!"

"Yeah, I keep hearing that." AJ said under his breath.

Ψ

Tony's SUV had been the ideal height for the discharge home; not low like Natalia's sedan, nor too high like AJ's pick-up.

The transfers to house and chair provoked some cramping, but not the feared, wracking pains that were scorched into his psyche before he had been carted from home to hospital, and still vivid in his recent memory. A front-wheeled walker had appeared; the riser toilet seat was in place. Copies of the daily and weekly schedule for physical therapy, medications, and follow-up visits were pinned up in the bedroom, bathroom, and kitchen.

AJ sat by his bed, leg extended, as home wrapped around him again. Something had changed.

"Sounds silly, but I put a little bell by the bed, one in the bathroom, and one in the kitchen so you don't have to yell for me." Natalia chuckled, displaying unexpectedly good spirits. "Gee, don't you get good service? But don't push your luck, buddy, or make me mad. You can't catch me now, you know!"

"Uh," AJ began, lamely. "Uh, I guess I need to thank you."

"Well, you got great care at St. Francis, and I'm certainly thankful," Natalia deflected. AJ's newfound civility rang hollow.

"Can you sit down for a minute?" AJ patted the bed next to him. "I have to say something."

Natalia cut him off. "AJ, I'm your wife. I'm going to take care of you. Don't say anything just for today or until you're back on your feet."

"Well, okay, I know. You've heard a zillion times how I'm going to change my ways, haven't you?"

Natalia pursed her lips, head tilted, with a steely-eyed confirmation of his stated premise. She crossed her arms, granting a momentary pause to see if there might be a kernel worth hearing, hoping for brevity or less.

AJ drew a deep breath. "I don't remember ever being so helpless, in so much pain, as when I fell. I'd never been so much at someone else's mercy. I've always underestimated you." An unpleasant chill shook him. "Men call out for their mommas when they're wounded and dying. I was at that point inside, lying on the concrete. And you showed up. I used to think of your staying with me was a weakness—nowhere to go, unable to fend. I now know that staying with me took incredible grit."

AJ's hand covered his mouth, aging eyes misted. Natalia turned, unimpressed by the late and effusive epiphany, even less so with his delivery. "Try to get yourself comfortable. I'll get you a sandwich and some soup for lunch," as she turned to leave the room.

"Wait, wait, please," AJ stammered. "Let me just say one more thing before I forget. I think you need to finally hear it from stupid me."

She paused to hear, one hand gripping on the door handle, ready to pull it closed behind her to cut off AJ's wheedling. She avoided looking back at him. Hanging her head spoke volumes to him of her exasperation.

"I do get it." AJ spoke quickly. "It's taken so long for me to get out of my own way and look around. About your teaching at the preschool . . . For years, people have been telling me you're some kind of genius, that without college or any sort of training, you have schooled nearly a generation of kids like a past master. The teachers with formal training take their lead from you! My god, that's got to be a calling. All those kids—so many come back to see you when they're grown up. No telling how you've affected their lives. You've got talent. That was your mission, and I never saw it. I wish I'd have paid attention. I've been blind to a lot of things happening around me."

She took the next step, drew the door closed, leaving without response.

CHAPTER 29
UNSPOKEN

The promised soup and sandwich would wait. Why was she being so accommodating to the ungrateful bastard? Why was she even listening at all? Unwelcome tears coursed her slender jawlines as she sat down at the kitchen table. Soft sunlight filtering through the dining room shades drew her into contemplation.

He's trying to say all the right things. Just how big a sucker does he think I am? Well, battered, belittled, and still around in her late sixties? What else is he going to think? I'm not a sucker! And anyone who thinks I am is wrong. I have stayed, for better or worse, because I chose to stay.

Through all the anger and tears between them, there had been an uncharted calculation, always with one or two points lead in the "stay" column. If I hadn't been smart enough to go to Al-Anon, it could have gone the other way. I have remained in control despite appearances. I have been true to myself, to my earliest moral convictions. I was supposed to look after my parents, no matter what. I was supposed to do my best to preserve my marriage and family despite the odds. And against all odds, I have succeeded!

It's obvious that AJ is still keeping score on my worth. So now, I got him through his worst nightmare! So now, I'm a great preschool teacher. So now, whatever else he can blow smoke about passes as some kind of big revelation. I know I am capable of a hell of a lot. I just look like a fool to the likes of him, because I don't brag. I know what to do, and I do it without fanfare. The proof of my life is in the pudding. Why didn't he leave? Because, underneath all the criticism, he's known all this and knew he couldn't find better. And yes, I've managed to keep him as the bread winner, because I've been in control, and leveraged this relationship to accomplish my goals. My papa and momma were taken care of, my children have grown up happy and successful, I kept my vows, and despite the bullshit, I'm a damn good teacher, in a school that brings out my natural talent. And, by god, I'm still here, and still managing!

I forgive. If I have any superpower, it's forgiveness. It's my secret weapon in the war to keep the idiots close, to keep myself half-way sane and half-way happy, and to avoid debilitating bitterness. Maybe forgiveness is why I don't have flashbacks! I'm no sucker, I'm just afraid of being called that. Well, fuck that fear! I make this choice each time and call in forgiveness to my advantage.

Is it even possible that AJ is just waking up to this after all the years and all the repetition? It is possible that at his crotchety age, he's having some kind of metamorphosis. Experience tells me this is just another post-drunk morning after, when he has conveniently forgotten all the abuse, and expects everyone to just be happy like him.

My resolution for the rest of my life—and everyone should hear my silent declaration—I know who I am, and I'm not changing. By the grace of god, I'm going to die happy and successful, as I see fit. And no one will take that from me.

I will be the good wife. If there is a revelation on AJ's part, I will take full advantage of that. I will take the praise, respect, and regard I've been earning all these years. I will forgive, and I will continue to choose my path. And if it is all falsehood, I will overcome that as well.

Ψ

Natalia switched on the kitchen radio to KRMG, the easy-listening from the sixties and seventies that Tony, the girls, and all their grandchildren would gang-up on her about. The wholewheat toast and her pasta fazool provided the ambient aroma, while she sped through the honey-mustard, avocado, tomato, lettuce, and turkey bacon layers for the sandwich. AJ had not asked for pain meds, and his appetite was back. Today's meals would be on a tray-table, and tomorrow's would advance to the kitchen setting. Not hungry yet herself, she brought a second glass of ice tea and sat while AJ devoured the goods, commenting in someone else's voice that this was the best meal he had ever had. The two caught up on family happenings he'd missed while in the hospital. She decided to try listening and remember the affirmative notions. She decided to let the love that had been there in past moments of intimacy and sharing to seep back through the cracks of her resolve.

CHAPTER 30
PATCHWORK

The late May sun was pure warmth, forestalling the weight of looming Oklahoma humidity. For now, the full flush of the radiant gardens of Woodward Park could be soaked up without regret; no one in the light crowd was in a hurry, except a few children chasing a border collie who delighted in eluding them. The inward trickle of families and couples from nearby neighborhoods continued nonetheless, in anticipation of the Memorial Day fireworks that would be visible in their arc from some grocery store parking lot on the restless ribbon, Brookside's main drag. Generations of Tulsa teens had amassed at weekends on that strip. The bursts would be comfortably audible and visible from Woodward, even before dark had swallowed the easterly horizon. For AJ, this comfortable distance from the celebration's pyrotechnics delivered more reverence to the meaning of the annual holiday.

"Really, is there no way you can stay here? Hell, this is the place you really got your legs, isn't it?" AJ handed Miko a cold, sweating, diet Dr. Pepper with a lime slice, partly obstructing the mouth of the slender bottle.

"Well, the rules are that you go back to your own country for three years before you can come back to the US, get a license, and practice on your own. You can get around that by taking a job in a seriously underserved area for a few years. But my mom is alone in Vathi. Our new baby will be good for her. The timing of the birth here will make him a citizen, however, so he'll actually have dual citizenship. If we want to come back eventually, we'll have several factors in our favor to get work visas and a green card." Miko took a long, satisfying first draw of the cool caramel fluid, ready to go on about the tedious immigration process. A burst of laughter from Bia and Natalia interrupted, as the one with the big baby bump was helped to a chosen spot on the grass, and the more senior losing her balance. Both rolled onto the lush green turf before pulling each other upright, in a girlish embrace, beside themselves, and each other.

"Thank you for getting together with us today," AJ began. "There's a lot I should thank you for. I hope this isn't uncomfortable for you, me having been a patient of yours."

"No, no," Miko replied to the overture. "You know, I was stunned when Bia told me that she and Natalia had met in a grocery store and kept their friendship hidden from us so there would be no trouble. Now Bia talks about Natalia so much, like she's a second mother or something. They seem to laugh all the time. I think it has been the closest relationship that Bia has developed the whole three years we've been in America. It's impressive that it was such a closely held secret while you were still a patient."

"Well, you know, Natalia's crazy about babies and watching them grow-up. She's nearly as anxious as Bia for the delivery, and at the same time, brokenhearted that you guys are leaving." AJ made a comical face toward the girls.

"Hey, this being our first," Miko said, "We're welcome all the help Natalia is willing to give. I hope that's okay with you."

"Natalia thrives on all the kid stuff, and she's good at it. It's good for her, too. She's really excited." AJ affirmed, vicariously.

"My mother and Bia's family are very excited, as well," Miko added casually. "Hey, you look good, AJ. How's it going for you?"

"Well, maybe Bia has told you by way of Natalia that, after you released me earlier this year, with my head on quite a bit straighter I might say, I wound up at St. Francis with a broken hip from a stupid fall. That's pretty much healed up as well. Oh, and last month, I finally did something I've been putting off for years—Natalia and I went to Washington, DC to see the Vietnam Veterans Memorial. I shouldn't have waited. It's this huge V-shaped slab of black granite with the names of all the fallen inscribed. It was emotional, even for Natalia, and a real honor for me."

"I've seen pictures of that memorial, AJ," Miko interjected, "and of the others from WWII and Korea. Those affirmations of a country's gratitude are so important for those who served and their families. I'm glad to hear it was a good experience for you."

"Since then, a couple more good things have developed since then, speaking of relationships. Would you believe an old man near seventy can fall in love with his wife again? Let me not get sappy, but I can hardly take my eyes off her. The sugary stuff and rough roads are behind us, at least I hope so. I'm a bit weird, but I find her amazing in ways I never noticed. She's a bit weird, though—my god, she always finds something good in every goddam nutcase she runs into, and everyone we see just flocks to her. All these decades and I never noticed. And without any sarcasm, she's led me back to the church. I'm no holy roller and still have a bit of a foul mouth, but it feels like I'm back in a familiar place from before I went off my rocker. Churches aren't perfect by any means, but they're big on forgiveness. We were married in the church. Boy, what a long, wicked ride it's been to be here now! Natalia stuck with me. I can't believe my good fortune."

"Take that good fortune and run with it," Miko grinned. "That's my street psychiatry for you today."

"So you'll be gone by the end of June, I guess. If one counted it all up, you'll be graduating from about the twenty-sixth grade, right?" AJ chided, grinning at the notion. "Have you enjoyed the time you've been in exile here? Gotten all you needed to get?"

"Frankly, AJ, it has been more than I could ever have expected," Miko reflected, energetically. "To be honest, there is a tendency for physicians to be drained of their compassion during these training years. I've been lucky. Our chief is a great teacher, you know, one of those unsung guys hidden away from the university research hospitals in relatively obscure places like this. He hasn't written much scholarly stuff, but is a master clinician, and a master at teaching and inspiring. Maybe you've heard from Bia and Natalia that a group of us residents is compiling a manual for future residents in psychiatry about managing the issues of vets. It runs parallel to conventional modern psychiatric constructs and infused with a trauma-informed approach learned from vets. I won't bore you with details. When it's done, perhaps I can send you a copy."

"Oh, yeah, me reading psychiatry?" AJ scoffed. "That would be rich, for a broken-down old salt like me."

"Hey, maybe it would help on those nights when you can't sleep!" Miko defended. "Anyway, the project has re-awakened for me a past hobby of writing. I think it helps with my own mental health. It's not the creative storytelling I once thought I might do, but I'm finding a lot of satisfaction from fashioning these human concepts into applicable words."

"Well good for you! I'm surprised you can learn much of anything from Vietnam vets," AJ quipped.

"Then you'll be surprised what other specialists have learned from them, and from their sacrifice." Miko commented more seriously. "Every medical student knows that shock lung was once called Da Nang lung, as it was noted and studied in the casualties from that war, as well as the first recognition that cholesterol arterial blocks from fatty diets can form in very young men, not just older people. Those were revolutionary findings!"

"That's more information than I need, Doc! Glad somebody is excited by it," AJ groaned. "Oh, that reminds me," he shifted. "There is something I wanted to give you as well, before you go. I brought it today." Settling his bottle on the low garden wall where the men were seated, AJ fumbled in the pocket of his windbreaker and drew out the emblematic shield. The patch, an embroidered coat of arms, remained tasteful and dignified, if somewhat rolling in at its margins and yellowed on its original white elements. AJ turned and presented the item ceremoniously to Miko with the fingers of both hands, as if it were a million-dollar check from the lottery.

"What's this, AJ?' Miko, grinned suspiciously. Resting his own cold one on the wall and wiping his moist palms on his pant legs. He accepted the offering politely, also with the fingers of both hands. Miko noticed AJ wasn't grinning; a sentimental gaze was fixed on the article.

"It's the insignia of the destroyer that I spent most of my Navy time on. Don't get all broken up over it, I've got a few more. Guys could affix this patch to anything the uniform code would allow. I know these women have exchanged a few little gifts, and your luggage is probably going to be stuffed with a lot of crap to haul back. I just wanted to give you something small. Maybe you would want to glue it to a magnet and stick it on your fridge or something," minimizing the obvious reverence he held for the insignia. "It's the coat of arms and motto.

'*Semper Confidens*' means something like 'always onward' from what I've been told. The tall ship is related to the *Waddell's* history; can't remember the details, but you could Google it if you want. Anyway, I wanted you to have something related to the two of us. My time on the USS *Waddell* did a lot to make me what I've been, for better and for worse. Anyway, I'd like you to have this. You can use it for ass-wipe on your flight home, if you want."

Miko frowned at the notion, shaking his head side to side. AJ continued. "You're important to me, you know. I know you'll just say it's your job. But, for the first time ever, somebody found me—you found me. Well, I guess you helped me find myself. The doors to all those silly rooms you talk about are open now, at least I think so. That's a construct I think I can keep organized in my small head," AJ assured as he gazed across the structured flowerbeds that dressed Woodward in the late spring. "Anyway, I'm going to keep trying to be a better man; maybe a little late, but hell, I'm not dead yet."

Miko scrambled for the appropriate response. "AJ, this is very nice, and very thoughtful of you. I don't know what to say. I'm honored, and no, I'm not going to wipe with it!"

Miko held the patch admiringly at arm's length and read the title banner aloud. "USS *Waddell*. You know, AJ, I know you mentioned the name of your ship several times, but I wouldn't have been able to name it now. Thank you." Miko noticed Bia watching the men from a distance and held the colorful patch at arm's length for her to see, taking a solemn pause in his chatter. "Where is the ship now, AJ?"

AJ glanced down at his unfinished bottle, reached and dropped it with its remaining contents into the nearby refuse receptacle. "Oh, well, she got decommissioned about six years after my tour of duty on her was over. She was mostly in dock for a few years. After that, she was sold overseas, and

I understand she, uh, let's see . . . ," AJ squinted toward the horizon and scratched his lower ribs as he did when searching his recall.

"She," Miko interrupted. "That reminds me of the first time when my father explained that boats were addressed as 'she' and were considered female."

"Yeah, he's right. Well, you might find this interesting. Don't know why I hadn't mentioned it, but she was actually bought by the Greek Navy, oh, I don't know, twenty or thirty years ago. She was old then, but they kept her in their green water fleet for a few years, and then she was sunk during active target training. Of course, she wasn't called the *Waddell* any longer after she left our fleet. The Greeks renamed her— something like Neercos or Narcos—something from Greek mythology or history, I think. I don't know if I'm pronouncing it right. Anyway, the guys I keep in touch with were grateful that the Greeks gave her an honorable demise like that, rather than scrapping her for metal. Kind of an emotional thing, you know." AJ furled his brow, after finishing the trivia he could remember.

The younger man felt a tingle on the back of his neck, as heat rushed to his face. "*Nearchos?*" Miko swallowed, his voice lurching, chest pounding. "Could it be *Nearchos*, AJ? *Nearchos?*"

"Yeah, *Nearchos*, I think. Why?" the question partly drowned out by the initial rumbling booms and skyward sparkles of the evening's spectacle.

ACKNOWLEDGMENTS

The universe works. Its entropy banged me into an array of accomplished and insightful folks like Valerie Davisson, Rod Scher, John Bingham, Kimberly Peticolas, and Norm Frani who each found me worthy of the pounding it took to get me to relate a story, away from the data, references, footnotes, and jargon of science writing. I am deeply grateful for their appraisals of value in the message and their patience in helping shape the delivery. Lastly, my wife Kell's unstinting critiques are the product of forty-five years of love, laughter, and soulful resonance.

ABOUT THE AUTHOR

P.K. Edgewater is the product of being the youngest of six siblings in a close-knit, blue-collar Catholic family, sojourns in seminary, military academy, and decades as a physician. Edgewater shares with readers his fascination with ordinary people and the courage and fears that map their lives.